AGAMEDE

A TALE OF MAGIC

GAIL B. SCHWARTZ

Castle Garden
Publications

Renton, Washington

Edited by S. C. Moore, C. E. Moore, and Emily Goldman.

Published 2014, Castle Garden Publications,
an imprint of Gazebo Gardens Publishing, LLC.
www.GazeboGardensPublishing.com

978-1-938281-41-9   (hardcover)
978-1-938281-42-6   (paperback)
978-1-938281-43-3   (e-book)

Library of Congress Control Number: 2013948998

Printed in the United States of America.

FOR MY PARENTS

TABLE OF CONTENTS

PART ONE:

MUMBAI, INDIA

AND

PORTLAND, OREGON

21ST CENTURY A.D.

CHAPTER ONE

THE FISHING FLOAT

When her parents first started talking about moving the whole family to India a few years ago, Mindy Fiddler thought they were totally crazy.

"It's halfway around the world," she'd said. "I'll miss too much school." That last statement was basically a smokescreen. At the time, Mindy was bored to death with school, but that didn't mean she was ready to pack up and leave.

"It's too good an opportunity to pass up," her parents had said. "India is a very exciting place. Besides, it's only for a few years."

It wasn't that she didn't want to travel. In fact, Mindy wanted to see the whole world someday—but it would be hard to leave her friends. At least she'd still have her big brother, Robert. He'd been her best friend in the whole world when they were growing up.

But, all that had changed the year after they'd moved to India—right after his thirteenth birthday. He thought he knew everything once he turned thirteen. He'd discovered girls—and they'd discovered him—and he hadn't been the same since. He'd always been such a sweet guy and suddenly he'd started getting into weird moods. Sometimes Mindy hardly recognized him.

Their mom said that it was just a phase he was going through because his hormones were racing. "He'll outgrow it," she'd say, "when he gets past puberty."

If we all survive that long, Mindy hoped.

Dad said, "He reminds me of myself when I was his age, and look how well *I* turned out."

Hilarious, Mindy thought.

"Call me when he grows up," he'd joke, and then take his newspaper into the bathroom and shut the door. That's when Mrs. Fiddler would roll her eyes and send for Ayah, their live-in housekeeper and nanny.

Ayah would take Robert out on the veranda for a little "chat" when he acted up, and when they came back in, he was always as meek as a lamb, at least for a while. Mindy didn't know how she did it. If it weren't for Ayah, their bungalow probably would've gone up in smoke.

Robert and Mindy used to spend all their spare time together imagining they were spies smuggling top-secret files, or astronauts exploring the depths of outer space. But after he turned thirteen, it was almost as if aliens had taken over his body, not to mention his mind. He spent practically every waking minute at the soccer field. What was even worse, his imagination had disappeared altogether. It would have been terribly irritating if it hadn't been so sad.

Mindy would never forget the day it happened. They'd planned an imaginary hunting expedition. They were to be Rajput princes searching the steaming jungles for a man-eating tiger that had been terrorizing the villagers for weeks. It was all arranged. The royal court was waiting.

The elephants—impatient to be off—were flapping their ears and stamping their massive feet on the ground, ignoring the soothing entreaties of their *mahouts*. Behind them, the purdah ladies were peeking out from the curtains of their elaborately decorated *howdahs* atop the smaller elephants, whispering and giggling amongst themselves.

Mindy had just adjusted her feathered turban and checked her rifle one last time when Robert had come out on the veranda and announced that he wasn't coming. There was an important soccer match that afternoon, he'd explained, and he didn't think he wanted to hunt tigers anymore.

"I know we've been planning this all week," he'd said, "but it's just kind of, well, kid stuff, if you know what I mean. And I have other things to do. Maybe you could find somebody from school to go with you." His eyes had shifted from Mindy's face to somewhere out on the lawn just beyond her right shoulder and back again.

In a split second, it was all over. The elephants and the

purdah ladies had disappeared, and her turban was once again just an ordinary old baseball cap with a feather stuck in the top.

She could have made a big scene, but she knew her brother pretty well—or she thought she did until that moment—and one look at his face told her it wouldn't do any good.

"You're going to miss the biggest tiger hunt of the whole season for a stupid soccer game?!" Mindy had asked incredulously. "That is absolutely the dumbest..." Then she'd stopped herself, because she didn't trust her temper. Instead she'd turned around and walked back inside the house.

She could feel Robert's eyes boring into her back. *Change your mind,* Mindy had pleaded silently inside her head, *please change your mind!*

"Sorry, Mins. I gotta go."

She'd heard his tennis shoes thudding down the steps, and by the time she'd turned around, he had hurdled the picket fence and was gone.

On numb feet, Mindy had dragged her way upstairs, but instead of turning into her room, she'd kept walking and found herself in Robert's instead. *What a slob,* she'd thought. She'd closed the door behind her and sunk down on his bed.

There were clothes and books and junk strewn all over the floor, but they looked like they belonged to someone she didn't even know. A crumpled soccer jersey lay next to her feet, and she had picked it up and buried her face in it. It smelled like sweat and India and the aftershave Robert had started wearing a couple of weeks before, even though he hadn't needed to shave yet. Like anybody cared.

At least Mindy's courtiers had full beards that smelled like musk and sandalwood, not just a few pitiful straggles like Robert, and they'd gone "hunting" with her any time she'd wanted.

"You still have us," they'd reminded her in her thoughts. "He's a jerk with a big ego and no imagination. You can get along without him just fine."

So when Mindy had heard a terrible sound, like somebody sobbing, it had taken a few seconds to realize that it was her. She'd tried to hold it back, but the best she'd been able to do was to hold the crumpled up jersey over her mouth and hope that no one would hear.

When she had finally stopped crying, she sat for a long time rocking back and forth, trying to arrange her thoughts. She hadn't wanted to just let it happen.

After that day, she tried to find a way to get him back, to make him her best friend again—something more exciting, more interesting than soccer and the silly, giggling girls who'd been following him around all the time. But nothing worked.

Mindy knew then that she had to accept her big brother was growing up.

Mindy was growing up too—she was twelve now, and Robert was fourteen.

Their family had moved to Mumbai, on the west coast of India, almost three years ago. Mrs. Fiddler was a visiting professor in computer science at the Indian Institute of Technology, and Mr. Fiddler was an ethnomusicologist studying Indian music.

From the moment their boat landed at Mumbai's teeming docks, Mindy had the strangest feeling that she'd come home, that she belonged in India. Everything about the place was like a fairytale—the hot air, the bright colors, the unimaginable sights and sounds, the unforgettable smell of a mixture of wood smoke, sandalwood, dung, and spices—and the people! Millions and millions of people, chattering in languages she'd never even heard of—Marathi, Hindi, Gujarati, Telugu, and Konkani.

Mumbai was India's biggest, most modern city, but like everything on the Indian subcontinent, it was full of contrasts—East and West, old and new, sophistication and superstition, gentleness and cruelty. India's rich and ancient culture had such a mysterious and magical feel about it. It was a place of spirituality and tradition with beliefs in karma and reincarnation—destiny and rebirth. There were cows wandering through the streets, even in the big cities, but no one made them move because people believed they were sacred.

In the countryside, holy men, with their faces and

beards grey from rubbed-in ashes, roamed from village to village holding begging bowls in their outstretched hands. Women with red caste marks on their foreheads drifted by wrapped in saris of scarlet, saffron, and purple, leaving behind the soft tinkling of tiny brass bells and the lingering scent of jasmine. Mindy loved the way their hips swayed back and forth as if they weren't connected to their bodies.

Sometimes when she was alone in her room, she tried to imitate that walk, but it was hard to watch her backside in the mirror and swing her hips at the same time.

There was also a sadness behind all the noise, color, and bustle in India, almost as if the ghosts of an older, grander era were hovering nearby, waiting to return home to a world that no longer existed.

When staring out her bedroom window at the city, Mindy often thought about back when she was in grade school. She had often found herself daydreaming when she was supposed to be studying. School had always been easy for her. Most of the time she'd been so bored, she'd imagined herself someplace else, just so she wouldn't jump up and run screaming out of the classroom.

When she was nine (it was during her piano-playing phase), Mindy had pretended her desktop was a piano. She was right in the middle of *Fur Elise,* when she'd realized that the room had gone completely quiet, and her teacher, Miss Guernsey—who looked just like a cow—was glaring straight at her.

"Bad listening habits," she'd announced in her sternest

voice, "will not be tolerated in this classroom. Anyone who believes *she* is too smart to pay attention may correct *her* thinking in the headmaster's office."

Mindy's face had turned red as a beet, which of course was exactly the reaction Miss Guernsey had wanted. After class she'd gone straight to the office and telephoned Mindy's mother.

"Really, Mrs. Fiddler, you must have a serious talk with Mindy. She is not paying attention when she should. She's always daydreaming."

"Oh dear," Mindy's mom had said. "Is she falling behind in her lessons? That's so unlike her."

"No, it's not that," the cow had said. "She's doing quite well with her studies, actually. It's just that so often she's just...well...someplace else."

"Yes, I know what you mean. I'll see what I can do."

So, Mrs. Fiddler had sat Mindy down for a little talk, and from then on, she'd kept her hands hidden in her lap at school.

Not too long after that, Mindy had stopped playing the piano altogether and begun her ballet phase. She'd gone in and out of a lot of phases. She'd start something, and then a few months later, she'd get bored and start something else. With so many interesting things to do, she couldn't pick just one.

Robert had said she never finished anything she started. Mindy disagreed. She had managed, however, to continually get herself into trouble with any sort of authority figure.

Her mother thought she did it on purpose, but that wasn't true either. It was just that there were so many silly rules. "Stand up straight." "Hold in your stomach." "Don't sing at the table." "Act like a young lady." And the one that had really driven her crazy—"Be CAREFUL, you might hurt yourself!"

Nobody ever told Robert to be careful, which was really why she'd been so annoyed. If Mindy had been born a boy, there would have been a whole different set of rules.

The last thing Mindy cared about was being somebody else's idea of a young lady. Once she started acting that way, she'd have to keep doing it all the time, and she had more important things to do—like having an adventure every single day, even if it was only a little one.

Sometimes when her parents were having dinner parties, Mindy would sit on the veranda outside the dining room and listen to them and their friends talk, or actually, complain. It was always something—the heat, their servants, their jobs. If that was what it was like to be grown up, why was everyone always in such a hurry to get there? Mindy just wanted to be left alone to do things her own way and in her own time.

"Ouch! What was that?"

"What was what?" Robert asked.

"Something heavy just ran into my foot. Hey, look at this," Mindy exclaimed.

Robert glanced up from where he was digging for sand crabs nearby and squinted against the sun as he wiped a few grains of sand off his nose. "Looks like a big old fishing float to me," he said, starting to dig again. "Why don't you throw it back? It's just a worthless piece of glass," Robert added.

"I disagree. I'm going to take it home. Maybe there's a secret message inside."

Humming to herself, Mindy came out of the water and rolled the ball up the beach, easing it along with her feet. She crossed over the clipped green lawn with its strutting peacocks and neat little rows of white croquet brackets, past Ayah, who sat fanning herself on the wide veranda, and up the front steps.

It was hard work because the glass ball was heavy, and by the time Mindy got to her room, she was hot and cranky. When she set it down at the foot of her bed, a silvery mist formed at its center, with little violet, pink, and blue lights darting in and out of the mist like goldfish in a lily pond. She knew then without a doubt that this was no ordinary fishing float.

She propped herself up with big fluffy pillows and glued her eyes to the float, scarcely daring to move. The house was completely still except for the hum of the ceiling fan—a soft, hypnotic swoosh, swoosh—and the faint buzzing of the little lights.

The heat and the silence wrapped around Mindy like a

cocoon, and she scrunched her eyes to keep them from dropping shut. By the time Ayah came in to check on her, she was sitting up in bed fast asleep, and the glass globe was as clear and lifeless as any fishing float.

It was the day after she'd found the strange globe at the beach, and her homeroom teacher, Mrs. Reed, came and stood right in front of her desk. Mindy didn't even notice her at first, and when she looked up, the whole class was staring at her.

Mindy was in sixth grade now, and she still had trouble concentrating in the classroom sometimes. There were so many other things a twelve-year-old would rather be doing than sitting at a desk all day.

"Mindy, you haven't listened to a thing all morning. Are you feeling all right?"

"Yes, Mrs. Reed, I'm fine, thank you," Mindy said, wondering if the globe's lights had really turned from pink to blue to violet and back to pink again, or if she'd only imagined it.

Mrs. Reed gave her a strange look. "Perhaps you'd better go home and rest this afternoon. We don't want you getting sick. I'll call your mother right after lunch."

"Yes, ma'am." Mindy slumped down and tried to look as pale as possible so Mrs. Reed would be sure to send her home. That way she could have the computer to herself all afternoon to do a little investigating. The sheer anticipation of it made her so excited, she could hardly sit still.

CHAPTER TWO

RAJA

On the day they'd arrived in India, Ayah had been waiting for them on the verandah of their new house with her bright black eyes alert as a bird, and her head cocked to one side in that way she had. Her snowy white hair hung in a thick braid down to her waist, and her quick, efficient movements reminded Mindy of the sandpipers that ran up and down the beach like miniature wind-up toys. Ayah hardly ever smiled, but when she did, her face crinkled in a million places and lit up the whole world.

Ayah had made it very clear to everyone from the beginning—including Mindy's parents—that as long as they were in her care, her word was law. It hadn't taken very long to learn that challenging her authority was totally useless. If you wanted to bend the rules, you had to find another way around, which was not an easy task.

So, when Mindy got home from school, Ayah had other ideas than computer time. It was hard to imagine how strong-minded she was, because Ayah was so tiny and fragile, that she almost looked like a child herself. But, she had raised four boys and four girls of her own and had very definite ideas about child rearing.

As soon as Mindy walked through the front door, Ayah fussed and clucked and then fussed some more. She tucked Mindy into bed straightaway with a cup of hot herbal tea and a cool cloth on her forehead.

"You stay put until suppertime, young lady," she said in her crisply accented English.

Mindy leaned back against the pillows and closed her eyes until the soft swish-swish of Ayah's bare feet on the wooden floorboards died away. Then she climbed out of bed and tiptoed downstairs through the silent house, past the sleeping servants, and into the study.

Behind the tightly drawn blinds, the study was dark, cool, and quiet. She switched on the computer and waited, tapping her fingers on the desktop. Patience was not her strong suit.

In a few moments, the PC sprang to life. Mindy knew right away that something strange was happening. Instead of the usual icons, a message appeared unlike anything she'd ever seen on the computer screen before.

Namaste, it read, using the traditional Indian form of greeting. Welcome to India Net, Miss Mindy.

This was really weird. The computer wasn't

programmed to know her name, and it *sure* wasn't programmed to carry on personal conversations.

<u>Namaste</u>, she typed tentatively in response. <u>Who are you?</u>

<u>My name is Raja. How may I be of service?</u>

Raja? Mindy's family didn't have a program called Raja. The hair bristled on the back of her neck.

At dinner the week before, she had heard Robert and her dad talking about artificial intelligence. Now, here she was, conversing with something—or someone—that didn't seem like a machine. It was like a presence of its own that lived inside the computer, but somehow completely independent from it.

Mindy's finger trembled over the power button. *Better not to mess with it, whatever it is...But what if I want to get it back and can't?*

It was scary but exciting at the same time. Clearly the thing to do was test it.

<u>Why are you helping me?</u> Mindy entered.

<u>I was summoned here to assist you with whatever you need.</u>

<u>Who summoned you?</u> Mindy asked.

<u>You must discover this for yourself.</u>

Very mysterious, Mindy thought. <u>I need some information</u>, she typed with fingers that seemed to belong to someone else. <u>Can you help me do a search?</u>

<u>Of course. What are you seeking?</u> Raja responded.

Mindy took a deep breath. <u>I found something on the</u>

beach yesterday, she typed haltingly. Something very unusual. I would like to find out more about it.

Ah yes, the spherical object that washed up in the tide at your feet. Very well, what would you like to know?

Only Robert and I know about the glass float! Mindy thought.

I wouldn't assume that if I were you.

How does it know? She wondered.

Sorry, I cannot reveal my sources.

What? Mindy hadn't asked it about sources. As a matter of fact, she hadn't spoken out loud! Could it read her thoughts? She decided to try something else.

Never mind, let's start with fishing floats, Mindy typed.

To her astonishment, the response came back immediately. And there it was, right before her very eyes. *A Complete Beachcomber's Guide*—pages and pages of information about fishing floats, their colors, shapes, and sizes, and how to tell a real float from a phony.

A genuine, hand-blown float will have little bubbles trapped in its surface. If there are no bubbles, it's probably not a real float, she read as she skimmed the page.

There's no mention of little colored lights, she noted. Interesting, Mindy entered, but that doesn't tell me everything I need to know.

Very well, I am at your disposal. Let us try again.

Then they tried, over and over, but to no avail. Mindy was beginning to run out of ideas.

Supernatural lights? Bioluminescence? Special

effects? Mindy typed in, reaching for ideas to explain the lights.

Come now, surely you can do better than that, the computer responded.

Mindy slumped down in the chair and chewed on the end of her ponytail. It helped her think. Maybe if she went through the alphabet the way you did sometimes when you couldn't find a word that rhymed...

Baseballs, bowling balls, crystal balls, fur-balls, masquerade balls, mothballs...crystal balls! Mindy shot straight up. Of course!

Why hadn't she thought of it before? Her float was perfectly smooth, with no bubbles or dents in the surface, which meant that it wasn't a fishing float at all, but something quite different. The only glass balls Mindy had ever seen that had lights inside them were the crystal balls you saw in the movies or at a fortuneteller's, which were supposed to be...MAGIC, she entered triumphantly.

Now you're cooking! Raja's response popped up on the screen.

There were thousands of entries. It took a long time to narrow them down, but eventually this was what she found:

MAGIC: branches of astrology, black magic, herbology, alchemy, mysticism, Kabbalah, Voodoo, Wicca, occultism and the supernatural, and parapsychology.

HISTORY OF: ancient Egypt, Australia, Celts, age of Greece and Rome, India, Medieval Europe, the twentieth century, and recent developments.

WHAT'S NEW: Sorcerer's Anonymous. conventions, organizations, covens, the Magician's Union, and World Wide Wicca.

PUBLICATIONS: *Who's Who in Magic Today.*

PERSONNEL: banshees, conjurers and sorcerers, demons and familiars, Druids, elves and fairies, mermaids and mediums, fortunetellers, ghosts and spirits, shamans, goblins and hobgoblins, leprechauns, gargoyles, gnomes and trolls, magicians, necromancers, priests and priestesses, sorcerers and sorceresses, witches and warlocks.

SHAPES: circles, mandalas, pentacles, and triangles.
TOOLS: altars, idols and images, amulets, charms, talismans, bed knobs and broomsticks, candles, computers, masks, wands, robes and fashion accessories, spell and incantations, and crystal balls.

Mindy clicked on 'crystal balls,' and a notation appeared: catalogues and supply houses, maintenance, operating instructions, upkeep and repair, warranties, history, and some additional information. She clicked on "history".

A BRIEF HISTORY: evidence of the use of crystal balls, both as purveyors of information and as tools for the casting of spells and other magical purposes, first appears in European texts as early as the eighth century A.D. However, references to their use in predicting the future do not appear until the early tenth century.

The first crystal balls were fashioned of quartz mined from desert caves outside the ancient, North African city of Alexandria over 2000 years ago, in what is now Egypt. Merchants brought the mineral by ship to Crystal Castle, the original Evillovich family residence on what is now the French Riviera. The quartz then made its way overland by caravan to the medieval Spanish town of Toledo, where master craftsmen fashioned it into the state-of-the-art crystal spheres prized by sorcerers and sorceresses around the world.

The Evillovich family controlled the crystal ball trade and was known at one time to be in possession of the most powerful crystal ball ever created, but its fate is unknown. Rumors hint that it may have found its way to North America sometime in the early twenty-first century when the last remaining member of the clan, Depravia Evillovich (who changed her first name to

Roxanne to fit in with modern culture), left France to live in the Pacific Northwest.

Crystal balls gained popularity steadily until the 1950s, when the invention of Plexiglas revolutionized the industry. However, it was the advent of the home computer era that signaled the end of this long and glorious chapter in the history of magic. The infamous and once-powerful Evillovich family then found its fortune and powers declining and fell into obscurity.

Crystal balls of today are primarily on movie sets and in the parlors of fortunetellers, who use magic-less globes to cheat a gullible and uninformed public.

By the time Mindy finished reading, she knew what she had found was a powerful crystal ball. *That must be why Raja is on our computer,* she surmised. *The crystal ball summoned him. But what am I supposed to do with it?*

She was completely lost in thought when Robert slipped into the study and snuck up behind her.

"Boo!" he shouted into her ear. Every once in a while, he forgot he was supposed to be a "grown-up" fourteen-year-old and acted more like a kid than Mindy did.

"Robert, don't *do* that. You scared me to death! Besides, Ayah will hear you."

"No she won't. She's napping like everybody else. What are you doing in here? I thought you were supposed to be resting."

"I can't sleep. You know that fishing float I found on the beach yesterday? Well, it isn't a fishing float at all, it's a crystal ball..."

"Wait a minute, Freckle-Face." Robert was always teasing Mindy about her freckles. "What are you talking about?"

"The *crystal ball*, the one that you said was nothing but an old fishing float. The computer helped me get information about it. It has magical powers."

"Yeah, right."

"It's true. See for yourself." Mindy pulled her chair aside so he could get a good look at the screen.

When he finished reading, he leaned back and let his breath out in a long, low whistle. "You really believe this stuff?"

"'Course I believe it. It's right there on the screen, isn't it?"

"Come on, Mins, you can't believe everything you read on the Internet."

"It was a magical program on our computer named Raja that helped me. That's how I *know* the glass ball is a magical crystal ball. And it has little lights inside it that flash and change color. Fishing floats don't do that. Come up to my room, and I'll show you." She sprang up and grabbed his hand.

"Mindy, hold on! I thought you'd outgrown all that imaginary games stuff. Besides, I have a soccer match in half an hour."

"Come on Robert—I can prove it. It'll only take a minute."

Robert sighed. Mindy could tell he thought she was being childish. But if she kept the pressure on long enough, sometimes she could still get him to do what she wanted. "Puhleeeeeze."

"Okay, but hurry up. I don't want to be late."

Mindy opened the door of the study just a crack to be sure no one was coming. Then they slipped upstairs and down the long corridor to her room. The crystal ball was resting just where she'd left it, on the woven rug next to the bed. It seemed to be dreaming. Its center, now a soft bluish glow, cast long shadows across the ceiling.

"So what do you want me to..." Robert stopped in mid-sentence.

They heard Ayah's footsteps shuffling down the hall. A moment later, she appeared in the doorway with her arms full of linens fresh from the laundry and her brown face radiating disapproval without saying a single word. She could do that better than anyone Mindy had ever met.

"I thought I told you to stay put," Ayah said, setting the linens down. "You get right back in that bed, young lady. Mister Robert, what are you doing here? You will be late for your soccer match. Go!" With a disapproving cluck, she hustled Robert out into the hallway and down the stairs.

As soon as Ayah's back was turned, Mindy gave the crystal ball a shove with her foot, sending it rolling safely out of sight behind her bed's dust ruffle. Then she jumped back into bed and pulled the sheet up to her chin. When Ayah came back, Mindy had her best smile on her face.

"That's better," she said, stroking Mindy's cheek. "I don't want my young lady getting sick. You must stay in bed until dinnertime, Miss Mindy, or your mother will be very upset with both of us."

"I will, Ayah, I promise."

CHAPTER THREE

ROXANNE

Roxanne Evillovich was hopelessly, deplorably vain. To be fair, her narcissism was not completely unjustified. In her prime, she had been the toast of Medieval Europe. No one knew her real age, of course, but she took great pride in the slender figure and tiny waist that had been her trademarks for more than a millennia.

Over the centuries, sorcerers and seers, peasants and prelates, commoners and kings, had all succumbed to her charms with devastating results. When her charms failed, which they seldom did, Roxie simply drew herself up to her full five feet, looked her opponent straight in the eye, smiled her irresistible, dimpled smile, and they were trapped—like a fly in a spider's web.

Like her infamous ancestor, Morrigan, the redheaded Celtic goddess of war, fate, and death, Roxie could assume many forms, from an old hag to an irresistible temptress. She preferred the latter, of course, because it showed off her beauty to its best advantage.

With the beginning of the Industrial Revolution, the world of magic had slowly begun to retreat into itself. Once the age of modern technology took hold, magic was virtually overshadowed and gone from the world. Those who practiced magic were few and far between, and their powers were mere shades of what they were in centuries past.

Roxanne Evillovich had once been one of the most powerful sorceresses in the world—but that time too had passed. She missed the covens, the spell making, the forces that came not from machines, but from the powers beyond human comprehension. She missed the adulation accorded her as a member of the most powerful clan of sorcerers ever to practice that mysterious craft.

In short, Roxie missed the profession she had loved for centuries. She found herself trapped in an ever-changing technological world that, despite its continual innovations, still lacked the glamour, the thrilling unpredictability, and the heart-stopping magnificence of a life dedicated to sorcery and the supernatural.

So, when the new millennium began, Roxie had taken a long, hard look at the family fortune and realized it was time to replenish it. She'd warehoused the most powerful of her mystical crystal balls and sold the rest, draped white sheets over the furniture in her castle on the Riviera, and headed for greener pastures in the United States.

She'd had no intention of settling in Portland, Oregon. In fact, she had never even heard of the place. But when her dear friend, Rasputin von Brunberg, offered her a tour up the Oregon Coast's Highway 101 in his private helicopter, with the family crest shining in iridescent purple on the tail, she'd accepted with delight.

They'd arrived in the Rose City at dusk, just as the city lights began to twinkle. They had banked over the graceful curve of the Marquam Bridge and the dark, green lawns of Waterfront Park with its tall buildings just beyond, when Roxie spotted what she now called the "Crystal Tower."

It wasn't the tallest building in town, or the most elegant. But its gigantic glass pyramid sitting on four smoky crystal-colored pillars atop the blue-tiled roof—lit up by teal and purple spotlights—gave it an ancient Alexandria look that immediately soothed Roxie's heart with memories of her family heritage.

Less than a week later she had purchased the building, moved into its magnificent penthouse suite, and installed living quarters for her staff on the uppermost floors. Once her furniture arrived from the family castle—an odd assortment of leftover remnants from former lives—she looked about her apartment and felt quite comfortable.

She named the building the Crystal Tower in honor of her family's former business and their castle in France. None of the customers who frequented it had the faintest idea who Roxie really was.

Soon she began buying up computer businesses around the world. She then proceeded to renovate the ground floor of the Crystal Tower and opened Roxie's Computer World, with a store grand opening the likes of which Portland had never seen. By the time she'd established the Crystal Tower as her international headquarters, with outlets and suppliers on six continents, she'd replenished the Evillovich coffers a thousand times over.

To the good citizens of Portland, she was simply the incomparable, if somewhat eccentric, proprietress of Roxie's Computer World, the busiest, most high-tech, state-of-the-art, hands-on technology store in the Pacific Northwest. Her reputation had quickly spread far and wide, and her sleek, space-age showroom with its neon lights and picture windows overlooking the Willamette River was crowded with customers from morning until night.

Roxie's clients adored her because she made them laugh, and despite her somewhat giddy demeanor, she was a shrewd, resourceful, and knowledgeable businesswoman who answered their every question and satisfied their every technological need. They sent her roses, expensive gifts, and tickets to the theater. She even held a seat on the City Council and was frequently seen dining with the mayor and his wife.

But, behind this charming and seemingly harmless persona lurked a creature possessing quite a different and infinitely more sinister nature. No power on Earth, or any other realm for that matter, had ever thwarted Roxie's plans once she'd set her mind to evil and her dark craft to work.

Now, after only a decade in Portland, and all her success in the computer industry, more than anything in the world, Roxie wanted to throw off the shackles of her entrepreneurial existence. She was miserable, unhappy, and wanted to restore the Evillovich name and herself in particular, to their former glory days.

So Roxie carefully crafted a plan. She would use the very technology that was responsible for her current miserable state to remake the world into a place where magic and sorcery were the most powerful forces once again.

Aided by her new prototype—a one-of-a-kind, magical computer software program she'd designed specifically for her magically enchanted laptop—she would use the Internet to truly wreak havoc around the world. She would spread viruses, reverse numbers, steal identities, start rumors, scramble e-mail messages and texts, damage documents, and destroy the economy. Soon the entire world would dissolve into chaos and pandemonium. There was so much evil and destruction she could cause. The possibilities were endless!

Just as she was about to launch this cleverest part of her evil plot, without so much as a whisper of a warning, obnoxious messages on her computer screen had brought her grand scheme to a screeching halt. They said things like, always look on the bright side, and, look for the sunlight through the clouds. And once or twice even, everything's coming up roses. Obviously something was dangerously amiss, and Roxanne, affectionately known by her colleagues as Roxie, was practically beside herself.

In fact, when the messages first appeared, she'd been right in the middle of her morning beauty routine. It was a daily ritual which she performed with the complete and utter joy that only an equally self-centered person could understand—if such a person existed, which was highly unlikely.

Now, her enchanted computer was down. Well, not exactly down, but certainly behaving in a most peculiar manner. And for a woman who prided herself on being the most high-tech sorceress in the Western Hemisphere, a computer malfunction did not bode well.

Roxie's auburn curls, usually impeccably coiffed, sprang out in undisciplined corkscrews around her head. Her porcelain skin, flawless save for a few freckles sprinkled fetchingly across the bridge of her nose, was mottled with rage. But the truly telltale sign was her eyes— those tip-tilted, Evillovich eyes had turned from their customary russet-brown to a menacing amber—a sure sign that Roxie was reaching the end of her patience. It was not a pretty sight.

By nine o'clock in the morning, she had tried everything she could think of, but no amount of rebooting, reprogramming, kicking, swearing, chanting, or incanting had the slightest effect on her enchanted computer. Roxie had been doing unspeakable things to other people's computers since computers were invented, but until now, no one had succeeded in doing the same to her.

Roxie knew that with the mere touch of a key and her newly created software up and running, she could take down the Internet, but no matter what key she pushed or what command she entered, Roxie couldn't get rid of the messages that appeared with increasing frequency across her screen. Count your blessings, the computer flashed cheerily. Honesty is the best policy.

"Count your blessings, indeed!" Roxie pushed the reset button for the hundredth time. "It's bad enough not being able to send messages out, but to look at this drivel all day is absolutely intolerable!"

She gave the computer desk a vicious kick.

I suppose, she thought, *I'll have to e-mail Rasputin for help. I'll never hear the end of it.*

Rasputin von Brunberg knew everything there was to know about building and repairing all types of computers— even enchanted ones. He was fascinated with them and sometimes preferred them to practicing magic. He was also a bit arrogant, as only a two-thousand-year-old sorcerer could be.

Rasputin@wizardry.com, Roxie typed out. Then she wrote a message. Raspy, Sweetheart, I'm having a bit of a problem with my computer. Be a dear and help me out. Come on over and we'll conjure up lunch. Yours, Roxie. However, when she hit the "send" button, something was quite amiss.

Sorry, all Internet pathways are temporarily busy. Good things come to those who wait, suggested the screen with irritating good cheer. Roxie hissed through her teeth as the screen offered, Have a nice day!

By now, it was half past nine and Roxie had accomplished nothing at all, not even a stock reversal. In complete frustration, she stalked over to the window to think.

From where she stood, she had a perfect view of the river's waterfront with its bridges and boats. It was a sparkling, clear day. On the far horizon, Mount Hood rose majestically into the sky like a proud, ermine-clad queen. Beyond Hood, farther still to the north, Roxie could see the smooth, rounded snow cone of Mount Saint Helens.

Sometimes people looking up from the street below or driving across the bridges wondered idly about the Crystal Tower's strange appearance, but they never dreamed—nor would they have believed it if they had been told—what Roxie was really doing up there in the penthouse suite.

Roxie sighed as she looked out the window, feeling the familiar ache in her heart for the good old days, centuries ago, when everything was so much simpler, and even the most elaborate scheme was merely a matter of...

"Of course!" she exclaimed. "Why didn't I think of it before? I'll get Rasputin to repair my computer and use my old crystal ball in the meantime, just to get things started. It may not be state-of-the-art, but it's reliable, even if it *is* a little slow."

Immensely pleased with herself, she strolled across the room and pulled out Pog, her gargoyle servant, from his favorite hiding place under the game counter where he had just settled in for a nap. Gargoyles were nocturnal creatures that simply were not at their best when the sun was shining—and this was a particularly beautiful spring day.

"Wake up, you lazy creature! I want you to bring my old crystal ball out of storage—and be quick about it! We have work to do."

Pog was slavishly devoted to Roxie, but at the moment he was not quite awake, so he just stood there looking at the floor.

"Well," she snapped, tapping her foot, "what are you waiting for?"

"Uh...to tell you the truth, Your Evilness," he ventured, "we don't have the crystal ball anymore. I mean to say...that is..."

"Don't have it? What do you mean we don't have it? That crystal ball is a family heirloom! It was a gift from my great-great—I don't know how many greats—grandmother, almost ten centuries ago. I distinctly remember making you personally responsible for its safe transport all the way from my castle in France to the Crystal Tower. Do you mean to tell me you *lost* it?"

"Not exactly lost it, Your Malevolence," he stammered, "but it is rather slippery, you know. I was flying across the river from the cargo dock as carefully as I could, and just as

I passed over the Saint John's Bridge, a huge helicopter swooped right down out of nowhere and almost cut off my wings! By the time I caught my balance, the crystal ball...I mean what really happened is...well, it dropped into the water. I'm so sorry, Your Wickedness, but I couldn't go in after it—I would have sunk like a rock!"

Roxie loved her view of the east side of the city and the Crystal Tower's location, so close to the river—but at the moment, it was an annoying reminder of the loss of her crystal ball. There was no time to waste. She pointed a long, well-manicured finger at Pog, and in the blink of an eye, his stony body turned into a statue. She'd have to hope Rasputin could repair her computer for now.

CHAPTER FOUR

THE COBRA

What Roxie had no way of knowing, of course, was that the crystal ball wasn't really lost at all. It was, in fact, miles and oceans and continents away, and quite safe.

Having narrowly missed a tugboat, it had landed in the water with a splash, popped back up to the surface, and begun its long journey down the Willamette River, its smooth surface glistening in the sun. It floated serenely by the mayor enjoying a morning canoe ride. It sailed majestically past crowds of smartly dressed diners enjoying breakfast on the terrace of the Waterfront Hotel. It passed under numerous bridges until it finally reached the mighty Columbia River.

Powerful currents then carried it westward until it reached the Pacific Ocean. It had wobbled and bobbled about on the high seas for quite some time, looking for all the world like a big Japanese fishing float—which is precisely what Mindy thought it was when it bumped into her as it came ashore on the beach of her parents' bungalow in India.

The next day was Saturday, and since there was no school, Mindy's plan was to spend the morning doing some more research. Usually on Saturday mornings, she and Ayah went shopping at the ancient bazaar. It was their weekly ritual. Ayah placed great store in rituals, so when it was time to leave, Mindy gave in to Ayah's urging and went along.

Normally Mindy looked forward to the trip because the bazaar, with its hodgepodge of makeshift booths piled high with mountains of fruits and vegetables and pyramids of sticky sweets, was one of her favorite places. Women from the nearby villages wound through the jostling crowds with huge baskets balanced on their heads as if they were permanently glued on. In all the time Mindy had lived in India, she had never once seen one of those baskets fall.

There were children everywhere, running between people's legs, playing tag, begging for *baksheesh,* and chasing each other between the booths while the merchants hissed and cursed and shooed them away.

Sometimes there were holy men walking back and forth over beds of hot coals or pushing long, sharp pins through their bodies. Ayah said they did it to show the power of mind over flesh.

But what fascinated Mindy most about the bazaar was the snake charmer, who sat cross-legged on the dusty ground in the middle of the square, playing his reed pipe. After a few bars, the lid of the big woven basket in front of him would begin to jiggle, just a little at first, then more and more until finally it flew off, propelled by something inside. A moment later, a king cobra would begin to emerge, inch by muscled inch, swaying rhythmically to the music.

When it reached its full height, almost as tall as a man, it would spread its gold and black hood and survey the crowd with terrifying implacability. The villagers, hypnotized by its flickering tongue and steely eyes, would stare back, swaying with it, rooted to the spot.

Mindy had seen the magnificent but deadly creature before, but on this particular day, something was different. As Ayah went off to do her shopping, Mindy advanced toward the cobra and it greeted her silently with a nod of its great, hooded head. Without thinking, Mindy brought her palms together in the ancient Hindu gesture of greeting and bowed slightly from the waist. As she looked into those dark, hypnotic eyes, she suddenly somehow knew that this particular snake was very old, very wise, and not at all dangerous.

"Namaste, Young Mistress," hissed the snake. "I have been waiting for you."

Mindy didn't know how or why she understood what it was saying, and no one else in the crowd seemed to notice their conversation.

"Namaste, Golden One," she responded.

"You must listen carefully, for I do not know when we shall meet again, and there is not much time. You have been entrusted with an important mission in which you must succeed."

Me? A mission? "What kind of mission?"

"There is a powerful force at work in the world, determined to wreak chaos and destruction upon humankind. You have been chosen to stop her."

Her? But who is she? Chosen by whom?

"That I cannot say. But know this. The one who you must stop is a powerful sorceress."

"Then how am *I* going to do that?"

"You will discover the means for yourself. Know, too, that you have power of your own, even though you do not yet know it. You must use it wisely and have faith in yourself, young one, as I do."

Mindy thought a moment. "Who told you about me? Does this have something to do with the crystal ball I found on the beach yesterday?"

No sooner were the words out of her mouth when the snake charmer abruptly broke off his melody and glared at Mindy from under his turban. The cobra bowed once more, drew in its hood and recoiled silently into the basket. With a flip of the wrist, the snake charmer snapped the lid firmly back in place. He tucked his reed flute under one arm and the basket under the other, and strode quickly away.

The startled crowd muttered its disapproval, but when the old man failed to reappear, they soon disbanded and dispersed to other parts of the bazaar.

Mindy looked up to find Ayah watching her with a strange, speculative expression in her dark eyes. Had she heard it too? Her face was impassive.

"Come, Miss Mindy," she said, leading her gently away with a hand on her arm, "it is time to go home."

CHAPTER FIVE

AGAMEDE

As soon as they got home, Mindy went straight into the library and booted up the computer.

Namaste, Miss Mindy, appeared the fluorescent green letters. How can I help you this morning?

Namaste, Raja, replied Mindy. I have something very important to ask you. The crystal ball I found on the beach yesterday...is it truly magic?

Is it real crystal or just Plexiglas? Raja asked her.

Good question. She'd never even thought about it. *It's very smooth and shiny and it has little colored lights inside it,* thought Mindy. I'm sure it's real, she confirmed.

Well then, Raja began, perhaps you should consider asking the crystal ball directly. They're usually quite friendly, you know.

How do I do that? inquired Mindy.

It is quite simple, but you must be tactful and try not to hurt its feelings. Crystal balls are delicate creatures. All those centuries of magic-making makes them rather sensitive.

Oh, I see, she thought. *I'll be careful. Thank you, Raja.*

My pleasure. Namaste and good luck.

Sensitive? Mindy could see this was going to be tricky. Maybe she should consult with Robert.

She raced up to his room and found him sound asleep. It practically took an earthquake to wake him when he was out like that, so Mindy took a flying leap for the bed and landed right on top of him.

He grunted and poked his head out from the jumble of blankets like a groundhog coming out of its hole. "Huh...what's going on? What time is it?"

"Eleven o'clock. Ayah is busy with laundry, and I want to talk to the crystal ball before she finishes. Come on!"

"You woke me up to talk to a piece of glass?"

"It isn't a piece of glass, it's magic!"

Robert stared blankly at her.

She could tell he thought the whole idea was totally crazy, but the one thing Mindy had to give him credit for was that he was a good sport. Besides, she knew he was intrigued, even though he would never admit it.

"Okay, okay, just let me brush my teeth. I'll be right there," he gave in.

A few minutes later, they met in Mindy's room. She pulled the crystal ball out from under the bed and placed it on top of the coverlet. Mindy's reflection stared back at her from the cool surface, distorted like in those crazy mirrors at county fairs.

"What do we do now?"

"We talk to it, only we have to be polite and respectful, because crystal balls are very sensitive."

"How do you know that?"

"I...I just know, Robert."

He sighed. "Okay, what do you want me to say?"

"Ask it...ask how we talk to it—and use a rhyme. Maybe it'll like that."

"Right. Okay, here goes nothing." He took a big breath and intoned in a deep, commanding voice, "Roses are red, violets are blue. Oh, Crystal Ball, how do we talk to you?"

Nothing.

"Sorry, I've never done this before."

"It's okay, try something else."

"Mirror, mirror, on the wall, how do we talk to you, Crystal Ball?"

"That's not funny," she said.

"Look Mindy, I don't want to burst your bubble, but I really don't think this is going to work. Let's go downstairs and have some breakfast."

"Not until we figure this out."

"Okay, then *you* talk to it."

All of a sudden, Mindy felt a little silly. What if Robert was right, and she was making a total fool of herself? But she had to do something. If nothing else, she wanted to prove to him that it wasn't a crazy idea, that maybe there really was magic in the world if you believed in it. Even if you didn't, that didn't mean it wasn't there, right? And if Mindy *could* prove it to him...

Suddenly, it hit her. If she wanted her relationship with Robert to go back to the way it was, all she had to do was to prove that the magic was real. That would be a hundred thousand times more exciting than all those stupid, goggle-eyed girls down at the soccer field.

Mindy bent down until her face was so close to the glass that her breath made a foggy cloud on its surface. "Namaste," she said gently, so as not to startle it. "Please talk to us. We need your help."

Still nothing.

Robert put his arm around her shoulder. "You know what, Freckle-Face? It still looks like an ordinary fishing float to me."

No, it can't be. That's not fair. "But it seemed so real. I swear I saw something."

"Hey, it isn't such a big deal. Maybe you just had a crazy dream. Come on, let's get something to eat. I'll make french toast."

Mindy could have hugged him.

Robert picked up the crystal ball and started to roll it back to its hiding place under the bed, when suddenly he yelped and dropped it like a hot potato.

There they were, the little lights, bumping around inside, only this time they were different colors—yellows, reds, and greens. Then suddenly, little bumps began to appear on its surface, and a moment later, it was twisting and stretching this way and that like taffy in a taffy-pulling machine.

By the time it finally stopped, it had shaped itself into a humanoid figure. More female than male, it was perfectly proportioned, with small, delicate features except for its eyes, which were two enormous and brilliant aquamarine gemstones.

Both Mindy and Robert stared at her in silence, trying to take in what had just happened before their eyes.

The creature stretched its newly formed arms and legs with a sigh of relief and looked around. "Thank *goodness*," she said in exasperation. "Whatever kept you so long?" the little being continued. "I had not had a chance to stretch in absolutely ages! And mind you, we do not have much time to sit around. We must act quickly if we are to stop *her*. Once you know the right words, you may wield my power. I do not suppose you happened to ask the cobra for the spell?"

"What cobra?" Robert asked.

"Shhhhhhh," Mindy quieted her brother. "Excuse me, but stop who?"

"Roxanne Evillovich. Do you mean to tell me you do not *know?* Good Heavens, this is even worse than I thought. Not to worry, of course, you will soon see that you are the right person for the job. But you must be very brave, because this will not be easy. You must do some travelling to find what you need. By the way, how is your medieval

Spanish?"

"My what?"

"Wait a minute, wait a minute," Robert broke in. "We're getting a little ahead of ourselves here. Maybe we should introduce ourselves first."

"Yes, of course, excuse me." The creature drew herself up proudly. "I am Agamede, unfortunately indentured to the Clan Evillovich, at your service. You may call me Aggie."

"I knew it! I knew you were magic! This is my brother Robert, and my name is…"

"Oh, I know who you are. That is why I am here, Mindy. You have the power to intercede. That is why you are the one who found me. When you picked me up on the beach, the power inside of you activated me. I had some magic in reserve that I used to draw you to me. You needed to discover magic for yourself, you see, so that I could reveal myself to you. You surely spoke with Raja, did you not? I created him to give you clues."

"Yes!" Mindy exclaimed. It was all beginning to make sense. "Raja helped me learn about crystal balls. And I also read about Roxie. But what is going on? What do you need me to do?"

"Roxie, that is Roxanne Evillovich, of course, plans to throw the entire world into chaos with her new, magical computer software program. I can sense her every thought with my magic, since she is a member of the Evillovich clan, and I am bonded to them. She will not stop there—oh no, far from it. I know her too well. I was in her service for centuries, and she cast me aside for modern technology. Thank goodness her computer is in need of repair at the moment, which gives us a little time, although not much."

Robert and Mindy sat listening in shock.

"Roxie was planning to use me for her evil plan until her laptop is fixed. As if a few microchips in a plastic frame could *ever* replace a genuine crystal ball. I do not know where she got such a silly notion. Probably from that insufferable sorcerer friend of hers, Rasputin von what's-his-name. He is quite enamored with the world's modern technology. In fact, I believe he may have taken a stronger liking to it than magic. Absurd!"

"Who's Rasputin?" Robert asked.

"Let me go back to the beginning of the story of my arrival here," Agamede suggested. "Two years ago, right after Roxie bought the 'Crystal Tower' building in Portland, Oregon, she sent for all of her belongings to be delivered to her new penthouse. Pog was entrusted with carrying me from the cargo ship to the tower to ensure my safe transport. On the way there, he encountered some difficulty."

"Who's Pog?" Robert interrupted.

"One of Roxie's servants. A gargoyle. He dropped me in the river, you see. That's how I got here—and a long journey it was, I must say. It quite wore me out."

"I see..." Mindy said, not really seeing at all.

"So now Roxie has all this technology—her computer, the Internet, the new magical program, and so forth—but she is unhappy, Goddess help us. I served her family faithfully for over two millennia, and how did she repay me? She packed me away in a dusty old warehouse and left me there, and now she wants me back. The sheer impudence! Well, if she is bent on mischief, she will have to go through me to do it. I would rather crack in half than help her."

"I'm sure glad you're on our side, Agamede," Mindy commented.

"Yes, but Roxie will not be an easy enemy to defeat. Of course, it is not her goals that truly concern me, you understand, it is her methods. I have watched these so-called modern inventions come and go for centuries. People just do not realize that there is no substitute for the real thing—real magic, I mean.

"The basic wisdom of the ages remains eternally the same. But, technology has advanced greatly, and people have come to depend on it. If Roxie succeeds in her plan to destroy the modern world as we know it, civilization will surely fall prey to chaos. That is why I summoned Raja to help, so you would be ready for my arrival—and to stall Roxie's plans."

"Right..." Mindy confirmed hesitantly.

"If you say so," echoed Robert.

"Good! Then we all agree. Shall we get to work?"

"What do we have to do?" Mindy asked.

"Well, first of all, it is not 'we,' it is 'you.' You are the one with the power, because you are the one who truly believes magic still exists in the world. Your brother, I am afraid, will have to stay home. Nothing personal," Agamede added as Robert's face fell, "but if one does not truly believe, nothing gets done."

Robert glanced at Mindy and considered contesting Aggie's decision, but then decided it was best not to speak against the ancient magical being standing before them.

"Secondly," Agamede continued, "we have a logistical problem. You see, I was commissioned specifically by and for the Evillovich family. That means that *normally*, no one but an Evillovich can fully activate my powers. To use my magic to stop Roxie, I must be fully activated. There is, however, a magic spell that releases those powers into the hands of the one who speaks the words to me. A written version of the spell *does* exist—but it has been lost. Most importantly, a crystal ball's power must be summoned while in the hands of the one who wants to use it. Do not forget this—it is very important."

"Is that where I come in?" Mindy asked.

"Correct! Your job is to find the spell. Once you have it, you can use it to summon me, and my powers, to your service. Then, together, we can shut down Roxie's magical computer program, or repair the damage she's done if she is able to set her evil plan in motion before you have returned with the spell."

"That doesn't sound too difficult. As soon as I find the spell, everything will be okay! Is your power really that strong, Aggie?" Mindy inquired gently, so as to not offend her.

"Ah, yes, indeed it is. I *am* one of the best, if I do say so myself," Agamede beamed. "Plus, do not forget that you possess great power as well. The problem lies in the fact that *finding and obtaining* the spell is going to be tricky—but we must succeed, as I cannot help you without it. And," she continued, "you must find it before Roxie figures out where I am and comes to fetch me."

"So *I* am the one who can stop Roxie?" Mindy asked. Her mind was racing. "Wow—a *real* magical spell! And we don't have much time, do we? Where should I start?"

"Well, let us begin with brainstorming possible locations of the spell—I do not suppose you happened to ask the cobra where it is? He is very knowledgeable, you know."

"No, he just said that I must use my power wisely, and then the snake charmer took him away."

"WHAT COBRA?" shouted Robert. "What snake charmer? What are you guys talking about?"

At that, Agamede instantly disappeared, and the crystal ball sat smooth and round in her place. Mindy and Robert stared at each other.

"Great, Robert, now you've hurt her feelings! You're not supposed to *yell* at her."

"Jeez, how was I supposed to know? Well, what do we do now?"

"I don't know. Try to get her to come back, I suppose."

But the damage was done. Agamede had retreated into the crystal ball like a turtle into its shell. After a few more tries, Mindy gave up—for the moment.

"Maybe she just needs some time to rest."

"Maybe she needs some time to pout," Robert countered. "She seems pretty temperamental to me. This whole thing is really crazy anyway—'talking' computers, a crystal ball, and now a little creature who wants you to save the world? *Right.*" Robert changed the subject. "Are you still in the mood for french toast? Come on, last one downstairs has to do the dishes!"

He was out the door in a split second, and after one backward look at the crystal ball, Mindy was right behind him.

That afternoon, they went for a swim at Mindy's favorite beach. The sea was very calm. She floated on her back, watching the big white clouds drift overhead while she tried to sort out her thoughts.

Mindy felt she had no choice but to help Agamede. If Roxie was threatening to use the Internet to create chaos and destroy the world's technology, she had to be stopped. That really would throw the world into pandemonium.

No computers—no way! Mindy thought. And then there was the damage Roxie's program would do to businesses, the banks, the economy...and it would bring so much more disorder than that—Mindy didn't even want to think about it. So, there was no way that if she could somehow prevent that from happening that she wasn't going to try.

But, there were so many unanswered questions. What did Agamede mean when she said Mindy would have to be brave? Obviously some sort of travel was involved. Would she be in danger? Where was she going? And how would she know what to do when she got there? This was all so strange and confusing—but also very exciting.

Only a couple of years ago, Mindy had wanted to have an adventure every day of her life and see the whole world. But the truth was, except for summer camp, she'd never been away from home all by herself.

Now it seemed that if she wanted to complete this mission she was being asked to take on, she'd have to go somewhere very far away.

The very thought made her stomach feel like there were a million butterflies fluttering around in it, trying to get out. She was old enough now that she no longer played imaginary games, but she did still believe in magic, and the thought of visiting new places and seeing new things was appealing. But what if she got into some kind of trouble? What if she got lost? What if she couldn't find the magic spell? What if...

"Mindy, time for dinner. Let's go!" Robert's voice jolted her back to reality.

She flopped over onto her stomach and headed for shore. For a moment, she felt calm, confident—ready for anything—until the butterflies came back and her stomach started doing flip-flops again.

One minute she felt like she was ready to take on the world, and the next she was terrified. It was totally unnerving, like being two completely different people at the same time and not knowing which one she really was.

As they began their walk home, Robert reminded her, "Don't forget, we have to start tomorrow morning no later than nine o'clock. The judges will be there at three, and I want to have plenty of time to get it all done, okay? Mindy? Hey! Earth to Mindy, do you read me?"

"Oh, sorry, I was thinking about something else."

"Well, pay attention, please, this is really important. Like I said, the panel will be here at three o'clock to judge the best sculpture. We have to be ready."

"Ready for what?"

"The Sandcastle Contest! Come on, Mindy, we've been planning this for weeks."

Mindy had forgotten all about it. The Annual Mumbai Sandcastle Contest was the high point of the season. People came from miles around to compete, or simply to gaze in wonder at the strange and extraordinary creations that arose like magic up and down the beach.

The temples, tigers, dancing girls, and flower-festooned elephants were so life-like, that sometimes it was hard to believe they were only made of sand. The winner's picture appeared the next day on the front page of newspapers all over India.

But Robert didn't care about that. All he really wanted

was the first prize—a candy apple red, twenty-four-speed mountain bike that was on display, all shiny and new, in the front window of the Mumbai Bicycle Shop. Every time they went into the city, he stood in front of that bike and stared at it with his eyes glazed over in awe.

If she could help him win it, Mindy reasoned, he would have to spend more time with her. And if being his partner in the Sandcastle Contest was what it would take to get his mind off girls and soccer, even for a while, then so be it.

His plan, using seashells and trellises, was to build a huge palace, like the one they'd visited in Jodhpur, with its tall towers, graceful arches, and delicately carved overhangs. Mindy was to be enthroned in royal splendor just outside the front gates, costumed as Razia Sultana, a young woman who had ruled Delhi for four short years in the thirteenth century.

Razia's father, a Turkish slave, had earned his freedom and become a great sultan. When he realized that his sons were too debauched to take the throne when he died, he passed the crown to his only daughter instead. The population had been outraged. Riots broke out in the streets at the thought of a woman on the throne, and a mere girl at that!

She was scarcely past her sixteenth birthday, but Razia astonished them all with her courage and intelligence. She wrote poetry, played exquisite music, spoke three languages, and recited the Qur'an by heart.

Razia ignored the advice of her counselors and rode

unveiled on elephant-back through the streets of Delhi with her glorious copper hair streaming down below her waist. Dressed in trousers and a turban, she quelled the riots, hunted, held court, and led her army into battle, sword in hand.

Mindy as Razia would be the final touch to Robert's masterpiece. Once they finished building the palace, Mindy had sworn to guard it with her life against the dangers of wandering cows and small boys with sticks until the judges arrived. A promise was a promise, so the crystal ball would have to wait one more day. Maybe it was a good thing, Mindy thought. At least she'd have time to do some planning.

The rest of the way home, she made a checklist in her mind of everything she would take with her, wherever she was going. Having a plan always made her feel a little better prepared.

Later that night, as she sat propped up in bed gazing out through the open shutters at the velvety, jasmine-scented Indian night, Mindy remembered something her mother had told her once. *"Be careful what you wish for. You just might get it."*

Mindy had wanted adventure. Now she wondered if perhaps she should have wished for something else.

CHAPTER SIX

MINDY'S QUEST

When Mindy opened her eyes early Sunday morning, she had the strangest feeling that Agamede had been waiting for her wake up.

"Good morning," came Agamede's voice cheerily from inside the crystal ball. Its violet lights sparkled as it rolled out from under her bed. "How are you feeling today?"

"I'm fine," Mindy answered. "I'm sorry about yesterday. Robert didn't mean to yell at you. Sometimes he just gets carried away."

"Well, it *was* a bit nerve-wracking, I must say. I am very sensitive, you know. But, no matter. I am quite recovered, and we have a lot of work to do. Come sit down here by me. I have something to tell you that may be a bit of a shock."

Mindy plopped down cross-legged on the floor to listen to Agamede.

"Roxie knows the magic spell, of course, but I can only be controlled when I am *in the hands* of the one speaking the words. That is why you must find the spell before Roxie repairs her computer or finds me and uses me for her evil plot. Unfortunately, the only place I can think of where it might be written down is in Toledo."

"Toledo? Toledo, *Ohio?* Why on earth would it be there?"

"No, no, no. Not Toledo, Ohio—Toledo, *Spain*, of course. The University of Toledo, to be exact. It was in medieval Toledo that I was crafted, and the spell to activate my powers was first created. You must speak with Don Lorenzo Alejandro de Carpio, Chair of the Department of Magic and the Occult Arts. If he does not have the spell himself, I am sure he can tell you where to find it. He knows a great deal about the Middle Realm."

"The Middle Realm?"

"That which lies between the world of the holy and the world of the everyday."

"Is that where I have to go?" *I think I might be getting in way over my head here,* Mindy thought.

"Perhaps, perhaps not. But enough questions. You must leave immediately."

Immediately? Mindy wasn't ready to leave yet! The butterflies started up in her stomach again.

She stalled for time. "Can't it wait another day, at least until after the Sandcastle Contest?

"I am afraid not. We have absolutely not a moment

to spare."

Mindy had to decide between helping Robert with the contest, or helping Agamede. As much as she loved her brother, she had been chosen—though she didn't know exactly how or why—to help stop an evil witch and her plan to wreak havoc on the world.

If I'm the "chosen one," the world may be in bigger trouble than Aggie thinks! But, Mindy loved the world just the way it was. So, her decision was made. She was going on a quest. *You said you wanted adventure, and that's exactly what you're getting. No chickening out now.* Mindy jumped to her feet. "I'll just grab my passport and pack a few things."

The crystal ball began to jiggle. The jiggling turned into shaking. The shaking turned into gales of laughter, until the ball was rolling around in little circles. The sparkling lights changed from violet to pink to a bright butter yellow. "Mercy!" Agamede exclaimed when the crystal ball finally rolled to a stop at the foot of the bed. "That was absolutely priceless. I have not laughed so hard in *centuries*."

"What's so funny?"

A sleepy voice floated down the hallway. "Mindy, are you all right? What are you doing in there?"

"I'm fine, Mom, I just tripped over something. Go back to sleep."

Mindy ran to the door and stuck her head out to be sure her mom hadn't gotten up. Then she picked up the crystal ball and checked it carefully for cracks before settling it gingerly up on a chair.

"You really *are* new at this, aren't you?" Agamede chuckled. "Well, my dear girl, you have a lot to learn. There has not been a Chair of Magic at the University of Toledo since the thirteenth century. As for your passport, I doubt very much they would have the slightest idea what to do with it."

"Then how will I...?"

"Do not worry about that," Agamede twinkled. "That is my job. Watch closely."

All of a sudden, the little lights began swirling again, only this time instead of blinking, they flashed like a thousand strobe lights going off everywhere at once. Even when Mindy covered her eyes with her hands, she could still see them—tiny spots of impossible brilliance forcing their way through her laced fingers and beating against her eyelids like enraged fireflies.

She felt something silky brush by her, but then it was gone. Light ebbed and flowed, and incomprehensible words were being whispered by voices all around her. Mindy was moving, but somehow not moving, feeling her skin, yet feeling nothing at all. And then it stopped as suddenly as it had begun, and everything was peaceful. A dappled pattern of light and dark flickered over her face, no longer brilliant and blinding, but gentle and soothing.

CHAPTER SEVEN

RASPUTIN

Roxie had decided to invite Rasputin to lunch in her penthouse suite in the Crystal Tower. Since her email hadn't been working, she had begrudgingly decided to release Pog from his frozen-stone state so he could deliver her message. Having lost the crystal ball and thoroughly upset his master, the gargoyle had been happy to comply. He had flown with determination to cordially invite Rasputin to a formal lunch with Roxanne. Delighted, he had accepted and arrived promptly.

This being a special occasion, Rasputin was dressed in his very best—a black tuxedo with an elegantly appointed purple vest, a wide-brimmed black cap lined with purple satin, and matching purple boots. His curly black hair, beard, and moustache were gelled to a high polish as befitted a sorcerer of his stature. Rings of onyx and moonstone glistened on each of his fingers.

At his waist, a wide silver belt with an enormous buckle sported the most important tools of a modern sorcerer's trade—a magic wand and a cell phone.

"Just in case," he confided to Roxie, tapping his belt with his fingertips.

Roxie was undeniably impressed with his appearance, although she would never dream of saying so out loud. *He may be a thousand years old,* she thought, surveying her friend from head to toe, *but when it comes to clothes, he certainly knows how to put himself together.*

After chatting over lunch about this and that, Roxie informed him of her computer problem. She didn't however, tell Rasputin the whole story. She showed him the strange messages that, unbeknownst to her, were Raja's part in Agamede's own plan to buy Mindy some time.

"I wanted to use my crystal ball to repair the damage," she fibbed, "but Pog put a wrench in *that* plan," Roxie scowled. "But no matter—it *is* lovely to have you here, Raspy," she cooed.

Roxie figured it was better to lie about the reason she needed her crystal ball. *The less he knows, the better,* she reasoned. *I simply can't have him interfering with my plan— his interest level in this world's wretched technology is far too high to trust him with the details.*

"Are you absolutely *sure* your crystal ball can't be recovered?" Rasputin asked. "I mean, how do you *know* it didn't float to the surface and wash ashore somewhere?"

"The thing's heavy—it's probably under five feet of mud by now," Roxie answered.

"My *dear* Roxanne, don't be so negative. We'll think of something," he reassured her.

"The only thing that would calm my nerves would be to find that crystal ball. Otherwise I'm sunk—unless you can repair my computer, Raspy darling."

"I'd be delighted to, my dear. But first, I brought my laptop. I've just installed a magical internal tracking system for supernatural items. It will determine the whereabouts of your crystal ball in no time at all. Wonderful thing, this new technology. Positively miraculous."

Roxie scowled at him.

"There you go being negative again," he chided her. Rasputin loved magic, but he was equally fascinated with human technology. "Wait, what's this?"

"What's what?"

"This! Come take a look."

Roxie glared over his shoulder, squinting her yellow eyes to see the screen.

"According to this report," he continued, the Evillovich Crystal Ball resurfaced a day or two ago off the coast of India. India, of all places!"

"What happened to it then?"

"I'm not sure, I can't quite make it out..." He entered more information into the laptop. "Aha!" he cried triumphantly. "Here we are. It seems that a girl found it on the beach and took it home with her."

"Took it home with her? That's easy then. I'll just send Pog to bring it back. What sort of girl is she?"

"Let's see," said Rasputin, beginning another search. With his magic program, he was able to come up with some surprisingly informative data describing the girl.

NAME: Mindy Gayle Fiddler

AGE: twelve

FAMILY: mother, father, brother Robert (age fourteen)

HOBBIES: music, chess, reading, computers, swimming

ACADEMIC STANDING: excellent

PSYCHOLOGICAL PROFILE: brave, creative, imaginative, highly intelligent, trustworthy, somewhat precocious, loyal, tendency to daydream, accompanying uncertainty about growing up

PHYSICAL CHARACTERISTICS: five ft. two in. tall, ninety-eight pounds, fair skin, blue eyes, red hair, freckles

"FRECKLES?!" Roxie shrieked. "She's got *freckles*?"
"Yes. Is anything wrong?"
"I should have known. I'm doomed!" she wailed,

flinging herself into the nearest chair. Roxie absolutely adored making a scene, the more hysterical the better.

"My dear friend, will you stop that silly caterwauling and tell me what in the world you're talking about?"

"She's a *redhead*, that's what. With freckles! Redheads with freckles are powerful beyond measure—even if they don't know it. And once they find out...well, I can't begin to tell you. Redheads are the troublemakers of history. Lizzie Borden was a redhead. Elizabeth I of England was a redhead. Madam DeFarge was a redhead in her younger days. Oh, this is terrible!"

"My dearest Roxanne, may I remind you that you're a redhead yourself and an enchanting one at that. With freckles, I might add. I simply don't understand what all the fuss is about." In fact, Rasputin quite adored Roxanne's red hair and freckles.

"Yes, yes, but that's how I know she could ruin everything! If she's a typical redhead, she's most likely able to figure out that my crystal ball has magic, and she won't hesitate to use it against me. We simply *must* steal it back before she does. And," Roxie added as the terrifying revelation struck her, "she might even use it to destroy my new software! There's not another program like it anywhere in the universe, and I have no backup for it. Once it's lost, it's lost for good, as is my plan to destroy the Internet, dissolve the world into chaos, and return to my glory days! We haven't a moment to waste."

"New software? World Chaos? Glory days?" Rasputin

questioned, knowing now that Roxanne had failed to share some significantly crucial information.

Roxie's eyes grew wide. *Great, I've blown it now. So much for keeping my plan a secret.*

"Ah, Roxie," he continued after a heavy sigh. "You never cease to amaze me. I see you have quite the plan!" *And I am far from fond of it,* Rasputin added in his head. *Destroying the Internet and causing world destruction will bring harsh consequences you may not be prepared to face.*

Better to keep that to himself for now, he decided. No use in driving her into a full-blown panic.

"But do not fear. I, as you know, am one of the most skilled sorcerers to walk the earth. And *you* are one of the greatest sorceresses that has ever lived. Surely between the two of us, we can handle one little schoolgirl, even if she *is* a redhead."

"You are absolutely right. How could I have been so silly? The first step is, of course, to repair my laptop—and then retrieve the crystal ball."

"Well, then let us not waste any more time. I shall begin working on your computer at once."

"Thanks ever-so-much for your help, Raspy, dear. I just *knew* I could count on you in a pinch!"

Rasputin smiled and nodded, but he was torn between helping an old friend and carrying out his *own* secret plan.

PART TWO:

TOLEDO, SPAIN

13TH CENTURY A.D.

CHAPTER EIGHT

HONI

When Mindy finally opened her eyes, she was sitting on the ground with her back against the rough bark of a tree. Above her head, shafts of sunlight broke through the leaves as they rustled in the hot, dusty wind. A wave of dizziness swept over her. She leaned her head back and waited for it to pass before rising unsteadily to her feet and brushing the earth and dried grass from her clothes.

The tree that sheltered her was an ancient, gnarled olive. It stood alone in the middle of a vast plain surrounded in the distance by a rim of harsh, utterly desolate hills, its dusty, khaki-colored leaves the only shade for miles.

High in the sky, a scorching white sun bleached all the color out of the landscape. *It must be noontime*, Mindy thought. Then she remembered with a start that only moments ago in India, it had been the cool of early morning.

How long had she been here? Was it even the same day? The same year? The same continent? She glanced down at her watch, hoping to anchor herself in time, and a chill passed through her. The hands were *gone.*

Mindy shaded her eyes with her hand and slowly turned around in a circle. Far to the south, atop an enormous rocky mound, the crenulated walls of a medieval city stood etched against a brilliant blue sky. From all directions, small groups of foot travelers, wagons, and riders on horseback made their way across the dry, inhospitable landscape, kicking up clouds of dust as they moved. As one of these bands came nearer, an ox-drawn wagon pulled away from the others and drew up beside her.

"May I offer you a ride to the city, young mistress?" the driver inquired politely, resting the reins in his lap. "Tis a long way, and the sun is exceedingly hot today."

Mindy looked up into the merriest pair of brown eyes she had ever seen laughing down at her from a sun-bronzed face framed by a wide-brimmed straw hat. Something about the way his face creased in a million places when he smiled reminded her of Ayah. "Oh yes, please!"

The driver bent down and offered his hand, and she grabbed it and scrambled up over the wheel onto the wagon seat. That was when Mindy realized she could understand him, though she somehow knew he was speaking medieval Spanish—and he could obviously understand her too.

"Thanks, Aggie," she said under her breath.

The friendly man was impossibly old—the oldest

human being Mindy had ever seen. His snowy white hair parted in the center and fell below his ears, and an equally white beard reached halfway down his chest. He was simply dressed in knee breeches and a linen chemise with billowing sleeves that tapered at the wrist, white hose, and loose-fitting boots. A pile of books and manuscripts with incomprehensible lettering embossed in gold on their leather covers rested on the wagon seat beside him.

He must be a great scholar, Mindy thought.

"Not a scholar," he stated with a shake of the reins and a cluck to the oxen. "Only a humble man of God." The wagon lurched forward with a jolt.

"But how did you...? I mean, I didn't...I hope I wasn't being rude." *How does he know what I'm thinking?*

"Not at all, not at all. Honi the Circlemaker, at your service, Miss..."

"My name is Mindy. Thank you very much for the ride, Mr. Circlemaker."

"My pleasure. You can call me Honi. Tell me, Mistress Mindy, what is a young lady like yourself doing in the middle of the plains of Toledo on so hot a day as this? And without a hat! Surely you are not travelling without an escort?"

"Yes I am. I'm on an important quest. I had planned to travel with my brother, Robert, but—he was unable to come along."

"And what is your purpose, may I ask?"

"I have to find the man who is the head of the

Department of Magic at the University of Toledo. You don't happen to know where that is, do you?"

"I might," said Honi, his dark eyes twinkling. "I might. If I may be so bold, precisely what is the nature of your business with the gentleman?"

"I'm looking for a magic spell. A friend told me he might be able to help me find it."

"A magic spell? That is very serious business. And what are you planning to do with this magic spell once you get it?"

"Well, I know it sounds pretty far-fetched, but to make a long story short, I'm trying to stop someone from throwing the whole world into chaos."

"Ah, now that *is* very serious business." Honi stroked his beard and gave Mindy a long, searching look from under the brim of his hat.

They rode along in silence for a time, listening to the clop-clop of the oxen's hooves against the parched ground.

"That is Toledo, straight ahead," Honi said finally, pointing his whip toward the city. "I can take you as far as the square. The University is right in the center of town. You will have no trouble finding it."

"That would be wonderful. May I ask you a question?"

"Not at all, though I cannot promise I'll have the answer."

"Why do they call you the Circlemaker?"

He chuckled. "Now that I *can* answer. Because that is what I do. I make circles, and then I stand inside them and ask the Holy One, blessed be He, for rain. Or for the rain to stop, or the crops to grow, or whatever the land and the people need. And the Holy One answers me."

"So that's how you knew what I was thinking! You're a magician!"

"A magician, no. Only blessed of God."

"But how...?"

"Ah, that is not important, Mistress Mindy. Just remember that you have been given great power, but you must use it wisely."

"That's exactly what my crystal ball said."

"You have a crystal ball?"

"Yes, that's how I got here."

"I see," said Honi, pulling on his beard.

"What I'd really like to know is..." Mindy began.

"Whoa there! Easy now!" Honi tugged on the reins as the wagon hit a rut in the road and lurched sideways. He cracked the whip to spur the oxen forward.

Suddenly Mindy caught a glimmer of sunlight on water up ahead.

"The Tagus," Honi explained. "Toledo was built at the bend of the river. We'll cross at the Bridge of San Martin."

Now that they were closer, she could see that the city was surrounded on three sides by a deep gorge, with shingle and grey rock running down to the water's edge. A cluster of stone mills lined the riverbanks. Their waterwheels sounded a lively clackety-clack in the fast-running current.

Soon they were in the midst of a great crowd of people, wagons, and carriages all converging on the main road to the bridge leading into the city. An equally noisy throng was pouring out, some herding flocks of geese, chickens, or goats, others driving wagons piled high with newly purchased goods. The sound of horses neighing, animals braying, people shouting, wagons creaking, and carriages rumbling was so deafening that Mindy could hardly hear herself think, so she contented herself with watching the panorama that spread out before them.

On the flanks of the hillside, an enormous fortress stood proud sentinel. "Alcazar," Honi explained. "The king keeps two thousand of his finest Arabian horses in its subterranean stables, ready to carry his knights into battle against the enemies of Spain. And that," he added, pointing the whip with a flourish, "is Toledo Cathedral."

Mindy directed her gaze straight ahead. There, rising from the very heart of the city, was the most magnificent, imposing structure she had ever seen, its delicate gothic spires holding up the sky.

The Bridge of San Martin, when they finally reached it, was an enormous stone affair of turrets and battlements. Toledo, oldest and proudest of Spanish cities, loomed stark and somber just beyond it, with its Christian, Muslim, and Jewish inhabitants going about their business.

At the entrance to the bridge, moneylenders weighed and exchanged the coinages brought by visitors from foreign lands. Vendors' booths lined both sides of the thoroughfare, piled high with bolts of damask and velvet, brass and copper pots, leather goods, weapons, and fine saddles. It was a strange place, both welcoming and sinister at the same time, as if the city wanted you to come inside and admire its beauty, so long as you didn't ask too many questions.

Once they were inside the city gates, Honi turned sharply to the right. The wagon plunged into the tortuous maze of impossibly narrow streets. Overhanging balconies, with their ornately carved wooden shutters, met overhead, shutting out the light and leaving the cobblestone streets in preternatural gloom.

Sometimes the streets seemed scarcely wide enough for an orange-seller to pass through, let alone an ox-drawn cart. But Honi maneuvered skillfully through a hundred twists and turns until they finally emerged into the bright, sun-washed square where the Toledo Cathedral soared skyward.

The cathedral dwarfed everything around it, an incomparable testimony to the grandeur of medieval Spain. An army of carved saints, sinners, demons, and dragons adorned its exterior.

Honi pointed upward.

By tilting her head back as far back as it would go, Mindy could see the huge rose window high above. The sun streaming through its intricate stained glass petals broke into a million tiny points of light that danced across the walls and floor of the vast entrance.

The square was alive with activity. A miracle play was in progress on the broad stone steps of the church. Merchants called out their wares, and magistrates conducted pressing matters of state.

Gentlemen with hooded hunting falcons perched on their arms promenaded for the ladies. Housewives exchanged the latest gossip while their men folk debated with endless good humor all manner of things about which they knew nothing at all.

Beneath the delicate tracery of flying buttresses that supported the cathedral's thick stone walls, master builders and artisans plied their crafts to complete the great edifice that their fathers, grandfathers, and even great-grandfathers had begun. A steady stream of serfs and peasants filed endlessly in and out, stooping under the weight of heavy baskets of timber and quarried stone while architects barked orders.

Far above the heads of the crowd, countless carved birds and beasts—the bizarre creations of fanciful and superstitious medieval minds—perched on every ledge and corner, surveying the commotion below with stony indifference.

Honi skirted the square, maneuvered the wagon down another long, narrow street, and came to a halt next to an ancient well. "Farther than this I cannot take you," he said. "You see that street yonder between the blacksmith's shop and the pottery maker? Follow it as far as you can, and it will lead you to the university. When you get there," he continued, "you must ask for Don Lorenzo Alejandro de Carpio. He is an old friend of mine, and perhaps he can be of help. But mind you, keep your counsel to yourself. The citizenry is highly superstitious and very suspicious of strangers. You must not speak of your mission to anyone, or you may be in the gravest danger. Do you understand?"

"Yes, sir."

"Oh, and before I forget, take this." Reaching deep down into his pocket, he drew out a long, golden chain with a dangling pendant. It glittered in the sunlight as he took her hand, dropped the chain into Mindy's upturned palm, and folded her fingers around it. "It is called a *hamsa*," he explained. "It will protect you against the evil eye."

"Thank you, Honi."

"And remember, promise me you will speak only to Don Lorenzo and no other."

"I promise."

"Get on with you, then. Good luck, my young friend. May God be with you."

With a cluck of his tongue and a flip of the reins, Honi turned the wagon back the way they had come. Mindy watched him until the ox-cart was completely swallowed up by the maze of dark streets.

All at once, she felt more alone than she had ever felt in her whole life. Mindy was hungry and thirsty after the long, hot ride, and the city seemed suddenly dark and sinister, despite the brilliant sunlight. It occurred to her that she had neglected to ask the crystal ball how to get home again. Panic knotted her stomach and tingled in her fingertips.

Then Mindy realized that she was still clutching Honi's gift. Opening her hand, she held the chain up to the light and inspected the charm. It was a delicately filigreed hand with a tiny blue enamel eye in the center of the palm. It looked very old. She fastened it securely around her neck and took a deep breath.

"Okay, Don Lorenzo," Mindy said aloud, mostly to convince herself, "here I come!" And she set out toward the University of Toledo and Don Lorenzo Alejandro de Carpio.

CHAPTER NINE

DON LORENZO

Mindy followed Honi's instructions as best she could, navigating the zigs and zags of the dark, narrow street until it dead-ended in front of an enormous stone structure with the words *Universita de Toledo* engraved in florid letters. An iron gate opened into a large, cobble-stoned square, with a marble fountain at its center from which four stone dragons rose on their hind legs, silently pawing the air with their claws. Plumes of water from their gaping mouths spewed high into the sky. She cupped her hands and drank in big, deep gulps, then wiped the dust from her face and sat down on the curved stone rim to rest.

The courtyard was completely deserted. Breathless heat hung in shimmering waves just above the pavement. On all four sides, long colonnades of graceful arches formed shaded outer corridors. Mindy followed one of them until she came to a heavy wooden door. She tugged on the handle, but it wouldn't budge, and her knocks echoed hollowly on the other side.

Retracing her footsteps, she followed the corridor in the other direction to where it, too, dead-ended at a wood door, also securely locked. She was re-crossing the courtyard when she noticed a smaller door partially concealed by shadows. Mindy grabbed its iron handle and pushed. It opened with a soft sigh, revealing a long hallway lined with marble columns.

High up near the ceiling, dust motes danced in slender beams of sunlight that penetrated the semi-gloom through narrow slits in the thick stone walls. After the heat of the courtyard, the interior was deliciously cool.

At the end of the corridor, she mounted a broad stone staircase that lead to the second floor, savoring the soft smoothness of the stone banister beneath her palm. At the first landing, a young man about Mindy's age dozed upright on a wooden bench with a forgotten manuscript on the floor at his feet. She considered waking him to ask where she might find Don Lorenzo de Carpio, but he looked so peaceful that she thought better of it. Instead, she picked up the fallen manuscript and placed it gently in his lap. He snored slightly and shifted in his sleep.

Mindy reached the top of the stairs only to find herself in another long, wide corridor lined with heavy wooden doors on either side, each firmly and forbiddingly closed. For the first time in her life, she regretted her fertile imagination. She thought of some of the stories she'd been told when she was a little girl—of the lady and the tiger, where opening one door meant life, and the other certain death, with no way of knowing which was which.

Her heart beat faster as she remembered *Bluebeard* and *One Thousand and One Nights*. What if she opened the wrong door and found a body, beheaded and dripping with blood? Or what if a ferocious beast with yellow eyes and razor sharp fangs waited to pounce and tear her flesh limb from...*Oh, stop it!*

Just to prove to herself that she wasn't afraid, she marched straight up to the nearest door and prepared to knock—then froze, hand in mid-air, as another door opened at the far end of the corridor. A man came out carrying a brass tray and whistling tunelessly to himself.

His eyes widened in surprise when he saw her, then narrowed with suspicion as he drew closer and saw the chain around her neck. "What are you doing here?" he demanded.

"Excuse me, I didn't mean to intrude, but there was no one downstairs to ask for directions. I'm looking for Don Alejandro Lorenzo de Carpio."

"What is your business with Don Lorenzo?"

"I...it's...uh, it's personal. I have a...a message to deliver."

"A message? From whom?"

"From...from a friend," Mindy stammered. "Please, sir, it's very urgent."

"From that heretic Honi the Circlemaker, no doubt," the man scoffed, taking in her appearance from the top of her head to her dusty tennis shoes. "You are obviously a foreigner. How do I know you are not a spy?"

"If I were a spy, I'd already know how to find Don Lorenzo. Spies know how to find people. That's their job."

"Is that so? My, we are an insolent little wench! Well, I am afraid it is quite out of the question. Don Lorenzo is studying and cannot be disturbed. Besides, little girls are not allowed here. Why are you not home helping your mother where you belong? Go on now, go away. Shoo!" He waved Mindy peremptorily aside, turned, and headed for the stairs.

"No, wait, please! You don't understand. I have to..."

"What is it, Stefan?"

An imposing man, elegantly but simply attired in a long, black linen tunic, emerged from a nearby doorway. Only a large silver pentangle hanging from a heavy chain about his neck broke the elegant austerity of his costume. He was clean shaven and very tall. His black, closely cropped hair and finely chiseled features reminded Mindy of the faces she'd seen in paintings by the great master, El Greco—dark, lean, and ascetic. His black eyes bored into hers as if they could penetrate her every thought.

The man called Stefan set down his tray, bowing deeply and respectfully from the waist. "Don Lorenzo. Please forgive the disturbance. This brash young lady insists she has a message for you, from Honi the

Circlemaker, I believe. I have told her you must not be interrupted, but..."

"It is all right, Stefan, you need not be alarmed. I shall take care of our young guest. Please, do not trouble yourself further." His voice was deep and resonant.

"As you wish, Don Lorenzo." With another bow, Stefan retreated down the corridor, casting suspicious glances over his shoulder at Mindy as he went.

"I am sorry," Don Lorenzo apologized. "Stefan is a good man, although perhaps a little overzealous in the performance of his duties. But no matter. You look as if you have had a long, hot journey. May I offer you something to drink?"

"Yes, thank you, I have come a long way. I'm searching for a magic spell for my crystal ball so that I can stop a great evil from throwing the whole world into chaos, and I don't have much time."

"I see," said Don Lorenzo slowly. "Unfortunately, I am not sure I can be of assistance unless I know a little more about your situation. Perhaps you had best explain it to me from the beginning." He ushered Mindy inside and gestured for her to sit.

While she seated herself in a big leather chair and examined her surroundings, he fetched a goblet of water and some fresh fruit from the wooden sideboard. She knew she was in the study of a scholar of magic and the occult, as the walls were covered in ancient maps, charts with cryptic symbols, pentangles, diagrams, and a circular drawing of the twelve signs of the zodiac. The enormous carved desk was piled high with books and manuscripts in Persian, Hebrew, Arabic, Latin, Greek, and some other languages she didn't recognize.

Don Lorenzo had been writing; a parchment half-filled with fine, florid script rested on the desktop in front of a blotter and inkwell from which a large quill pen protruded. On one corner of the desk sat a human skull, and on the other, an hourglass. A globe of the world hung suspended in a heavy, wooden stand next to the desk. On the wall directly behind the globe hung a picture of a hand exactly like the one Mindy wore around her neck—fingers pressed together and a blue eye in its center radiating beams of light.

She was studying the hand so intently that she was nearly startled out of her wits when she heard a loud *CAW!* directly behind her. Mindy turned to see an enormous, shiny, black raven perched on the back of Don Lorenzo's high-backed chair.

It cocked its head and regarded her with a baleful, yellow-eyed stare. "CAW!" it croaked again.

"Do not mind Lady Alice. She looks fierce, and her manners leave something to be desired, but she is actually quite harmless."

"Oh, I like birds." Cautiously, Mindy stretched out her hand to stroke the glistening feathers.

Suddenly coy, the crow lowered its head and peeked up sideways like a playful child.

"See, she likes you too."

"Why do you call her Lady Alice?"

"She is named after a woman whose serving maid was the first person in Ireland to be burned at the stake for witchcraft. Consorting with the devil, the court said."

"How awful. Was she guilty?"

"Oh no, and neither was her mistress. It seems that Lady Alice's greatest crime was outliving her first three husbands and inheriting their considerable wealth. When her fourth husband went insane, her stepchildren proclaimed that she was a witch and denounced her to the authorities. They wanted her money, you see. Of course, Bishop LeDread was only too happy to oblige. He had just arrived from England to establish the Inquisition and was anxious to assert his authority—and what better way than by striking terror in the hearts of the citizenry? Lady Alice fled the country with her life, although very little else, I am afraid. But the Inquisitors wanted their pound of flesh, so they arrested her serving maid, that poor innocent soul."

"I don't understand how people can do such horrible things."

"Ignorance, fear, superstition. We live in dangerous times. One does not actually have to do anything to be accused of witchcraft. Of course," he added matter-of-factly, "all of that does not happen for another hundred years. But, as you probably know, seeing as you are a time-traveler yourself, time is relative, especially in the Middle Realm." He smiled at Mindy's obvious astonishment. "Now," he continued, seating himself opposite Mindy behind the desk,

"Stefan said you were sent by Honi the Circlemaker. Honi and I are old friends. When did you last see him, and how does he fare?"

"I only just met him this morning. He gave me a ride into the city and told me where to find you. And he gave me this." She showed Don Lorenzo the *hamsa*.

"Have you shown this to anyone?"

"Stefan saw it. I think it scared him."

"I am not surprised. Honi frightens people, quite unintentionally, you may be sure, but frightens them nevertheless. He has a very special gift, which they do not understand. We call it the Third Eye, the ability to see truths others cannot see. With these truths, he is able to change the natural order of the universe. Or rather, he does not change the universe himself, for none of us can do that, but he calls on the Higher Power to change it."

The Third Eye...that must be what the eye on my necklace represents, Mindy realized.

"There are many things in this world that we cannot explain," continued Don Lorenzo, "because they come from the Middle Realm, which few people know anything about. Of course, all esoteric knowledge is very powerful, which is why I teach my students to use what they learn only in the service of good. Even so, the population here is mostly uneducated and superstitious. I should not be surprised if one day the Department of Magic will be dispensed with altogether by the Church. I have already received complaints from the Town Council and threats from the citizenry as well."

"What would you do then?"

"Oh, I do not know. Retire to the country with Lady Alice, perhaps. She is quite a wise, old bird, you know, and excellent company."

"So is my cobra. Wise, I mean. Well, it isn't exactly mine, but it did speak to me in the bazaar, so I sort of think of it as mine. We seemed to understand each other. I mean..." She was sure he must think she was crazy, prattling on and on about a talking cobra. But he only looked intrigued.

"What did your cobra say exactly?"

"He said that I have great power and must use it wisely."

"Then you must be a very special young lady, indeed."

"I don't know about that. I only know that if I don't find the magic spell soon, Roxanne Evillovich will carry out her plan and the entire world could dissolve into complete chaos. I thought about 'abracadabra', but it seemed so silly."

"No," Don Lorenzo, clarified, "abracadabra is an incantation to heal the sick. You start with the whole word and shorten it, letter by letter, until all the letters are gone. Once they disappear, the illness disappears as well, assuming, of course, you know the rest of the words to say with it. It is never so simple as merely one word. Otherwise, it would be much too dangerous."

From a pile of parchments weighted down by the hourglass, Don Lorenzo extracted a large chart and pushed it across the desk toward Mindy for her to look at.

ABRACADABRA

ABRACADABR

ABRACADAB

ABRACADA

ABRACAD

ABRACA

ABRA

ABR

AB

A

"Hmmm. That's very interesting, but I don't think it will work for my crystal ball."

"I am afraid not. By the way, we used to make them here—crystal balls, that is. Many years ago, when I was still a young boy, the University of Toledo employed a master craftsman who shaped the most elegant and powerful crystal balls in the world. His technique was a secret, of course, as was the nature of his work. The poor fellow was betrayed by one of his own apprentices and was drawn and quartered in this very square. When he died, his secret died with him. Your crystal ball would not happen to be an Evillovich by any chance, would it?"

"Yes, that's what I've been told," Mindy confirmed.

"Ah, I thought it might be. The Evillovich clan privately commissioned all of their magical accessories; nothing but the best would do. Their crystal balls were particularly fine. To be sure, the Wikovskis, a rival clan, also produced quite a nice model. But when the family fortune changed, they sold their factory and went into alchemy instead, a great pity. But all that is really of no consequence. Tell me, why have you made this journey all by yourself? Was there no one to accompany you?"

"My brother, Robert, wanted to come with me, but Aggie—that's my crystal ball—said he couldn't because he doesn't believe in magic."

"Ah, that would be very problematic."

"Yes. He thinks that believing in magic is silly."

"Oh, but it is not the magic that you really believe in, you know. Although, of course, it always helps to believe."

"It isn't? What is it then?"

Don Lorenzo smiled. "Yourself. Once you believe in yourself, you can do anything. The magic only helps you along. In fact, believing in yourself is the simplest, most reliable magic I know. Did Honi not tell you that?"

"No. I never thought of it that way before."

"Perhaps he wanted you to discover it on your own." Don Lorenzo leaned forward on his elbow and his fingertips pressed together. He studied Mindy for several moments in silence.

Finally, he seemed to reach a decision. "If we are to find your magic spell, we must search the archives. I keep some of my books here in my study, but there are others that contain knowledge so hidden and profound that they must be guarded carefully, to be used only by those with enough wisdom to use them properly. I keep them locked in a secret place. You must swear that you will never tell anyone you have seen it."

"I swear."

"Good. Let us go, then. Yes, of course, you can come too," he added as Lady Alice hopped onto his shoulder with a protesting *SQUAWK!*

Don Lorenzo rose to face the *hamsa* on the wall and pressed the eye at its center. Slowly, silently, the stones behind it swung backward to reveal an unlit, circular staircase. Taking a lantern from the nail next to the stairwell, he led the way down the narrow stone steps. As soon as they entered the stairwell, the hidden doorway swung shut behind them without a sound.

CHAPTER TEN

WITCH HUNT

Down and down they descended, round and round until Mindy's head was spinning. She had to cling to the iron railing to keep her balance.

When they finally reached the bottom, Don Lorenzo led the way into a labyrinth of dim underground passages. Finally, he stopped in front of an iron doorway. The threshold was so low that even Mindy had to bow her head to enter.

She had expected to find herself in a small, monk-like cell. Instead, the room in which they now stood was a cavernous, subterranean chamber lined with row upon row of books and manuscripts, their faded, dusty covers embossed with gold lettering that glimmered faintly in the lantern light. An odor, peculiar and ancient, but not unpleasant, hung in the stale air.

"Incense, she said, wrinkling her nose against the musty smell.

"Wisdom," responded Don Lorenzo, "the Wisdom of the Ages."

He hung the lantern on an iron hook in the wall and strode to one of the bookshelves from which he extracted several volumes, choking on the little puffs of dust that arose from their ancient covers. Soon, he was completely immersed in his task.

He read for what seemed like a very long time while Lady Alice, perched on his shoulders, shifted from one foot to another like a restless child. "Patience, my darling," he soothed, absentmindedly stroking her dark head.

Carefully, he turned another yellowed page and scrutinized its faded, carefully inscribed symbols and diagrams with a practiced eye. When he had finally finished the last manuscript, he returned it to its place and turned toward Mindy with a sigh. "I am very sorry," he said gently, wiping the dust from his hands. "I am afraid the spell is not here."

"But it has to be here! If it isn't, I've come all this way for nothing, and I can't possibly go home without it. Besides, I don't even know how to get home." Mindy could feel her throat close up and begin to ache the way it did when she felt like she was going to cry and didn't want to.

"It seems to me," said Don Lorenzo thoughtfully, "that the spell you seek may be found somewhere much farther away." He considered her, thinking to himself. "Are you prepared to undertake another journey?"

"I...I think so. Where would I have to go?"

"To Avalon. Have you ever heard of it?"

"We read about it in school. It's a mythical place, isn't it?"

"Some say so, others believe it really exists. According to legend, Avalon is an island far to the east, near India I believe, hidden in the mists of the Summer Sea. Within its boundaries, there are no wars, no one grows old, and no one ever dies. It is part of the Otherworld, where everything is possible and great deeds are accomplished. The island is ruled by Morgan le Fey and her nine sisters. Morgan is also, I might add, half-sister to the legendary King Arthur. Like her brother, she grew up under the tutelage of Merlin, the great wizard of Britain."

"What makes you think she might have the spell?"

"Morgan is a Druid priestess, a powerful sorceress and mistress of healing arts and magical arts in her own right. She can transform herself into a bird—shape shifting it is called—and foretell the future. But she only shares her powers with those who journey from afar to seek her counsel. Since you fit that description quite admirably, I see no reason why she would not assist you."

"Wait a minute. Didn't you say this place is off the coast of India? That's where I just came from."

"Yes, but Avalon exists out of time and space, and no one can travel beyond its mists unaided. The only person I know who can get you there is Honi the Circlemaker. Before you make the journey, however, you must rest. Doña de Carpio and I have plenty of room. You can dine with us this evening if you like and stay the night under our roof. Tomorrow morning, we will find Honi and send you on your way."

"That would be wonderful. I *am* really tired." As a matter of fact, Mindy hadn't realized until that very moment just how tired she was. "In fact, I feel sort of jetlagged. It must the time travel."

"I beg your pardon?"

"Jetlag, you know, when you…" What was she saying? This was the thirteenth century. Jets hadn't been invented yet. "Never mind, it's just a figure of speech."

"Oh. Well then, it is settled. And do not despair. We will find your magic spell."

They retraced their steps and re-emerged into the study. Don Lorenzo was just gathering up his books and charts when there was a tremendous commotion from the square below.

They ran to the window. The sky was aflame with the orange and crimson light of the setting sun, and the man she recognized as Stefan was standing on the edge of the fountain inciting a mob of armed townspeople gathered around him with angry words and gestures. At the end of his every sentence, they roared their approval with a shaking of fists and brandishing of weapons.

Nearby, a tall, muscular man in a black executioner's hood stood motionless, his burly arms folded across his chest, while a third man piled dry logs and kindling around a wooden stake. Clearly an execution was about to commence.

"They're talking so fast, I don't understand. What are they saying?" Mindy asked.

Don Lorenzo leaned forward, straining to catch the words. "Dear God!" He drew his head back inside the window before he could be seen. "They are looking for you! Stefan has told them you are a witch. You are to be burned at the stake for heresy. Quickly, we have no time to lose!"

The sound of voices and running footsteps in the corridor signaled that it was already too late to escape through the hallway. But by the time the door burst open a moment later, they were already through the hidden door and down the spiral staircase.

Don Lorenzo lead the way through the subterranean passages with Lady Alice clinging to his shoulder, until they passed through a small doorway into a long, thin tunnel that stretched steeply away into blackness.

In their haste, they had left the lantern behind, and it was slow going because the walkway under their feet was wet and slippery with moss and loose stones. They had to inch their way forward, hand over hand, along the clammy stone walls. The air inside the tunnel was stale and cold.

After what seemed like an eternity, the ground sloped upward again and they emerged into an uneven street far outside the university walls. Mindy drew in a deep breath of fresh, wind-warmed air and leaned against the wall to rest for a moment, but Don Lorenzo was off again.

"This way!"

She was about to follow when he suddenly turned around, grabbed her arm, and pulled her into a narrow space between two houses. Torches flared at the far end of the street.

"There they are!" a hoarse voice shouted. "After them!"

"Listen to me!" said Don Lorenzo. "The only safety to be found in Toledo this night is in the cathedral—you must take sanctuary there. Continue down this street, turn left at the apothecary, then left again at the smithy, and you will see the spires. Keep them always in your sight and stay in the shadows as you go. I will remain here and talk to the townspeople."

"But..."

"No arguments, you must go quickly. Do not worry about me. I have calmed them before, and perhaps I can do so again. I will join you later if I can. Now go. Run, as fast as you can!"

"Goodbye, Don Lorenzo! Goodbye, Lady Alice!"

"Goodbye, my child. May fortune be with you."

With a flap of her jet-black wings, Lady Alice spiraled up and away until she disappeared high above the rooftops. Mindy took one last look at Don Lorenzo standing tall and alone on the cobblestones in the path of the oncoming mob.

"Go!" he urged.

She turned and ran.

The angry voices gradually died away behind her as

she made her way through the darkened streets. But as she rounded the comer of the apothecary shop, she almost ran smack into another mob. It seemed as if the whole city was looking for her.

Mindy plunged into an alleyway, scrambled over a fence, and dropped down on the other side, scraping both knees so badly they bled. She raced on and on until her heart was jumping out of her chest and she couldn't take another step.

By the time she finally stopped, she had completely lost her bearings. The overhanging porches, so charming and quaint in the daylight, now leaned menacingly inward as if to bar her escape.

Voices and the glow of torches seemed to come from every direction at once. Mindy tilted her head as far back as it would go and turned slowly around in a full circle. All she could see was the smallest possible patch of night sky as velvet black as Lady Alice's wings. *The spires,* she thought. *I can't see the spires!*

The panic that swept over her was so powerful that her knees gave way. How foolish she had been, how arrogant to think that she could undertake this mad adventure and save the whole world when she couldn't even save herself.

Now here she was, lost in the thirteenth century with no way home. Unless, unless... Mindy's mind raced. "Think, think! There has to be a way!" she whispered frantically.

Then she remembered the *hamsa.* Her hand flew to her

throat. Thank goodness, it was still there.

"You have great power," the cobra had said. *"You must use it wisely and believe in yourself."*

Don Lorenzo had been right. Mindy understood now that the power she possessed was the ability to believe in herself. But, until this moment, she had never really tested it—because she was afraid of failure.

"You never finish anything," Robert's voice mocked her. And it was true. Mindy had always been afraid that if she tried, really tried, she might fail. Only this time, there was more at stake than just her ego.

With all the strength she could muster, Mindy clasped the amulet with both hands and willed herself to block out everything except Honi with his flowing white beard and his books piled high on the wagon seat beside him. Like a mantra, she began to repeat his name under her breath, lulling herself into a gentle trance, the way Ayah had taught her to relax when she was stressed out.

Honi the Circlemaker. Honi the Circlemaker. Honi the Circlemaker. Honi...

"CAW!" With a soft swoosh, Lady Alice swept down from the nearest rooftop and landed on Mindy's shoulder.

"Oh, Lady Alice! Do you know where...?"

"Do not be frightened, my young friend," came a familiar voice. "We have come to take you to the cathedral. Mind you," added Honi, emerging from the shadows, "this is not going to be easy. It seems the whole city of Toledo is looking for you. And me," he chuckled, as if he found this vastly amusing.

"Honi, thank goodness you're here! It worked—you heard me!"

"I did indeed, though 'twas Lady Alice who showed me exactly where to find you. But come, we must make our way to the cathedral, and quickly. The cart is nearby."

The next thing Mindy knew, they were hurtling headlong through the narrow streets with a pack of baying dogs in their wake. The wagon lurched frantically from side to side, scraping the walls until sparks flew from the wheels. As they neared the cathedral, the light of hundreds of torches converging on the square lit up the night sky with an ominous glow.

Honi drew the wagon to a halt. "We will go by foot from here. There is a back entrance through the cloisters where the monks come and go. No one will see us."

They made their way through the maze of small shops and makeshift lean-tos lining the outskirts of the cathedral until they came to the monks' quarters. Silently, they passed through the narrow iron gate and down the graveled path that lead through the kitchen gardens, entered the side door, and slipped inside.

Then Mindy stopped, transfixed. Never in her life had she seen anything so magnificent, so unearthly, so utterly overwhelming as the interior of the Toledo Cathedral. The vaulted ceiling—supported by columns so thick that a dozen men with their arms outstretched could scarcely reach around them—was so high that it was completely lost in shadow.

Rich tapestries and paintings decorated the walls. An opulent velvet canopy embroidered with gold and silver threads and studded with seed pearls adorned each bay and chapel. Atop each altar, with its drape of delicate, snowy-white Spanish lace, bejeweled wine goblets and holy relics glistened dimly in the reflected light of a thousand votive candles. Wraith-like clouds of incense from carved braziers overhead hung suspended in the still air.

But the crowning glory of the Toledo Cathedral was the high altar at its center and the magnificent reredos that rose behind it, with layer upon layer of canopies, niches, and figurines intricately carved in white stone.

Under a glittering field of stars in a deep, blue sky that stretched into infinity, a grand procession of saints and churchmen, angels, and soldiers marched upwards towards the heavenly throne, bearing the proud standard of the Spanish nobility. In their dazzling presence, Mindy had never felt so impossibly small or utterly insignificant.

She would have stood there for hours if Honi hadn't beckoned with a frantic wave of his arm.

"Come girl," he whispered hoarsely. "This is no time for sightseeing!"

Taking her by the elbow, he propelled her toward the central nave until they stood directly beneath the dome. There, he extracted a piece of white chalk from the pocket of his breeches and drew a large circle, placing Mindy squarely at its center.

Next, he marked the four points of the compass—north, south, east, and west—and carefully divided the circle into ten sections, labeling each with letters and numbers, and muttering under his breath.

As he worked, the commotion outside grew louder and louder, like approaching thunder, until suddenly, the furious pounding of fists against the massive wooden doors broke the gloomy hush of the interior.

"Honi, they're almost here!"

"Patience, child. The circle must be properly drawn or 'tis of no use whatsoever. Besides," he added, calmly surveying his handiwork from beneath bushy, white eyebrows, "I have never done this before. You must help me all you can and stand very still."

For a moment, Mindy could scarcely believe her own ears. "What do you *mean* you've never done this before? You told me you were an expert. You told me you could bring rain and make the crops grow!"

"And so I can. I have done that many times before. But transporting someone to a different time and place, well now, that is an entirely different matter. I did not even transport myself here, truth be told."

"I thought you lived here."

"No, indeed. I am a time traveler like yourself." He smiled the sweet, guilty smile of a child caught in a lie with the best of intentions, but a lie nevertheless.

How Mindy recognized that smile! She'd used it more than once herself, and she knew how it felt on her face.

We're doomed, Mindy thought. She took a deep breath, counted to ten, and forced herself to stay calm. She looked him right in the eye. "Okay. If you don't live here and now, where did you come from?"

"From a time and place long, long ago. The first century before the birth of Jesus Christ, to be specific. And once we have sent you on your way, there I shall return."

"Oh fine, that's just great. Do you mind telling me how you got here in the first place if you don't know how to do this?"

"Why, you summoned me. Sometimes it is in our darkest moments, when we don't know where we will find the wit or wisdom to go on, that we find our greatest strength. When you first arrived here and were friendless and lonely, you needed me, and so you called me forth. Do not worry—it will all make sense to you in time, as you learn more about your own powers. Meanwhile, it does not always have to make sense, does it? Sometimes one simply takes these things on faith. Nothing ever gets accomplished without it, you know, nothing at all."

"I still don't see..." Mindy said, her eyes pleading for further explanation. But her words were lost as the pounding fists gave way to a battering ram that shook the cathedral to its very rafters.

They both froze. With a great splintering of wood, the doors gave way. The enraged mob, with Stefan in the lead, surged forward toward the central nave and up the aisles.

"There they are!" he shouted, and others behind him

took up the cry.

"Surround them!"

"Grab the old man!"

"Seize the witch!"

Mindy looked for an escape route, but there was none. Clearly, there was nothing to do but follow Honi's instructions.

With the crowd closing in, she stood still, scarcely daring to breathe while he finally completed the circle to his satisfaction. Then he stepped inside, raised his arms, palms upward, and lifted his eyes to the heavens.

"Maker of the Universe!" he shouted, his voice surprisingly strong and clear above the din. "You who hears all, sees all, and knows all, hear my plea. Remove this young seeker from the path of danger and carry her to Avalon so that she may complete her mission and return safely home."

No sooner had he spoken, when an enormous vacuum sucked all the sound from around them into the center of the circle. Mindy could see people running toward them with their swords and hatchets upraised and their mouths open and shouting, but there was no noise, no footsteps, no clatter of weapons. The very molecules in the air around them had frozen.

Then out of the silence, Honi's voice came again. "Maker of the universe, hear me! I will not move from this circle until you have answered the call of your humble petitioner. Spirit of the earth, *hear my plea!* Spirit of the sky, *hear my plea!* Mighty ruler of the Middle Realm and all that dwells within and between—HEAR MY PLEA!"

Mindy and Honi both felt it at exactly the same moment, a mighty rumble that began deep within the bowels of the earth and spread upward and outward until the flagstones shook beneath their feet and the great, vaulted ceiling trembled.

Incense braziers swung crazily from side to side. Goblets and candelabras tumbled from the high altar to the stone floor with a tremendous clatter. The rose window rattled and shook.

The enraged men and women pouring toward the nave with their weapons upraised froze in their tracks and stared about, wild-eyed with terror.

Then, all at once, they threw their weapons to the ground, turned, and ran blindly out of the cathedral, stumbling over each other in their haste.

Within seconds, the church was completely empty except for Mindy, Honi, and Lady Alice. Even the priests had fled.

"It worked!" she shrieked, jumping up and down and clapping her hands. "Honi, you're a genius. They're all gone! Now we can..."

But when she turned to hug him, his kindly, weather-beaten face had begun to spin before her eyes. Soon, the entire cathedral was whirling like a top and Mindy was spinning with it, turning and turning, faster and faster. Colors and candlesticks were careening madly out of control. Columns, rafters, and flagstones were all topsy-turvy. Faster and faster and faster—until they seemed to spin off the very ends of the earth—and then everything went black.

PART THREE:

THE ISLE OF AVALON

SOMEWHERE IN TIME

CHAPTER ELEVEN

AVALON

Something soft brushed Mindy's cheek. She opened her eyes slowly, because she was still dizzy from all the spinning, and looked straight up into a thick canopy of pink and white apple blossoms. Beyond them, the pale, silvery disk of a full moon hung suspended in the night sky.

The heavy scent of incense still clung to her clothes and hair, but the air was cool and sweet with the smell of flowers and fresh earth. Where was she? Then she remembered that Don Lorenzo had said Avalon was famous for its fruit trees, especially apples. A lovely thought, until a more sobering one rushed in to take its place. If Mindy was indeed on the Isle of Avalon, she was also in a magical, mystical place that didn't really exist—and no one knew she was here.

Her family must have discovered by now that she was

gone. They were probably crazy with worry. Even if Robert explained about the cobra and the crystal ball and the magic spell, they'd never believe him in a million years, and why should they? He didn't really believe it himself. Besides, he probably wouldn't even tell them because they'd think he was certifiably insane. Mindy just wanted them to know she was safe.

The sooner she completed this quest, the better. She jumped up and brushed the petals from her lap. If this was a magical place, and Morgan le Fey really was the magical person she was supposed to be, Mindy should have the spell and be home by dinnertime the next day, no problem.

Obviously the first order of business was to find Morgan. She looked around. A narrow footpath led from the orchard through a fern thicket into the forest beyond. The woods were thick, dark, and strange.

Mindy had only gone a few paces when she had the unmistakable feeling of being watched. Somewhere unseen, dozens of eyes peered out from the shadows, following her every move.

The back of her neck began to tingle. The eyes could belong to anything—probably not humans, but strange, magical beings from this place. What had Don Lorenzo called it? The Middle Realm. Mindy began to worry that strange, horrid creatures or twisted little gnomes would trap her with their spells and enslave her in their enchanted kingdom under the hills forever...

Oh, for Heaven's sake, Mindy, stop it!

Sometimes her imagination was like Pandora's Box—once she opened it, even just one tiny crack, all kinds of nasty, unspeakable things popped out. *Think of something else,* she admonished herself. *Think about the bazaar, the Sandcastle Contest, anything. Think about home.*

High above her head, a night bird called out, and somewhere far ahead and out of sight, another answered. Were they announcing her presence? Mindy turned slowly in a circle, scanning the underbrush.

Nothing moved in the unearthly quiet. Then, as suddenly as it had come, the feeling was gone, and there was nothing but the thick, soft carpet of pine needles beneath her feet and the night wind caressing her cheek. *Don't be childish,* she chided herself, and kept walking.

Soon Mindy spotted a glimmer of moonlight on water among the trees ahead. She veered off the little path and picked her way through the underbrush until she reached the shores of what appeared to be a cove encircled on three sides by a wide, pebbly beach.

The still surface gleamed like a burnished mirror. Far out from the shore, the lake was enshrouded in an impenetrable, pearl-grey cloud. She crouched in the tall reeds near the water's edge and waited.

A moment later, a dark shape began to emerge from the mist, until at length, a great barge appeared and glided toward her, travelling utterly without sound. Pale circles of light rippled and danced as the oars sliced silently through the glassy water, but Mindy could see no one at the oars. In fact, there didn't seem to be any human presence onboard at all, almost as if a powerful and invisible force was propelling the vessel.

As it drew nearer, unseen hands unfurled two banners from its prow. The first bore two golden serpents intertwined against a field of dark blue with a crescent moon, and the second, a red dragon rampant against a field of white.

Suddenly, a blessedly humanlike voice rang out in the stillness. "Yonder lies the shore!"

"The shore!" came the response from a dozen grateful throats, and all of a sudden the decks burst into pandemonium. With a bump, the barge scraped up on the gravel only a few yards away from Mindy.

Someone lowered a pair of gangplanks off the starboard bow, and a small band of soldiers and horses began to disembark onto the moonlit beach. They were followed by a hay-filled cart and four men bearing a litter, which they placed in the cart with great care, as if it was bearing a person of great consequence.

Mindy poked her head above the reeds as far as she dared to see who it might be, but it was impossible to tell.

One of the soldiers bent down and spoke soothingly to the person in the litter. "'Twill not be long now, Your Majesty. We are safe here. Search as they might, your enemies will never find us here."

"And even if they could," added his companion, "no one would dare to invade Avalon."

If the litter's occupant answered, the words were lost in the commotion.

When all had come ashore, the barge slowly withdrew, turned, and glided back across the lake as smoothly and silently as it had come. The small band of men stood quietly shoulder-to-shoulder and watched until it disappeared once more into the mist.

"Come lads, it's on to the Lady of the Lake!" someone shouted.

With much chattering, clanking, and slapping on the back, they gathered up their equipment and prepared to march.

Mindy wasn't about to pass up this chance to be led right to Morgan le Fay, the woman she had come to find. When the soldiers headed out with the cart in the rear, she clambered over the side and burrowed beneath the hay. It was scratchy and smelled of horses, but the air had turned chill, and at least it made a warm, cozy hiding place.

She must have been more tired than she realized, because within minutes, the gentle rocking motion of the cart lulled Mindy into a deep and dreamless sleep.

CHAPTER TWELVE

KING ARTHUR

It was still night when Mindy awoke. She had no idea how long they had been traveling. Slowly poking her head out from beneath the hay, she saw that the moon was at its zenith.

They had emerged from the forest and were moving through a broad, brightly lit meadow of tall grass dotted with bluebells, foxglove, and starflowers. On the other side, a complex of modest but beautifully constructed wooden dwellings sat nestled within a ring of pale, silvery birch trees.

They came to a stop in front of the largest structure, a tall, shingled building with a pointed roof completely covered in wild primroses. Someone had thrown the entryway wide open, and a warm, buttery light flowed out across the grass. Silhouetted in the doorway, with her arms raised in welcome, stood the tiniest, most delicate woman Mindy had ever seen.

The first thing she noticed was that the woman's hair, unbound and flowing in thick rippling waves past her waist, was as red as her own. In her flowing white night shift and dark blue robe with its wide, billowing sleeves, she seemed not so much to walk as float, every movement graceful and ethereal, yet full of purpose and strength.

She went immediately to the litter and greeted its occupant in a low, pleasant voice. "Arthur, at last! Goddess be praised, we have been so worried. You and your men are most welcome. Are you in pain?"

"'Tis not so deep as a well, nor so wide as a church door, but 'tis enough, 'twill serve." The reply was good-humored, but the voice was weak and strained. "My memory fails me. Who wrote that?"

"It comes along sometime in the fifteenth century. William Shakespeare, I believe."

"Yes, of course, Morgan, I remember now. Well, no matter."

So she is *Morgan le Fey!* Mindy thought.

"We must take you inside and dress your wounds at once."

"But my men?"

"Will be well tended by my handmaidens, I assure you," she assuaged him. "Do not speak further, Arthur, you must save your strength. Now that you are here, all will be well."

Mindy remembered vaguely from school that King Arthur, having been mortally wounded in battle, fled to Avalon with his most loyal knights to seek his sister's healing powers. But what happened then? Did Morgan nurse him back to health? Did he die?

Try as she might, she couldn't remember. That had been during Mindy's drawing phase, and she was too busy doodling to listen to Miss Guernsey drone on about Arthurian legend. She wished now that she'd paid more attention.

No matter. She was clearly in the right place, and now all she had to do was speak with Morgan. But she'd have to be very careful. After what had happened in Toledo, Mindy wasn't particularly anxious to call attention to herself.

"You are all welcome," Morgan said to Arthur's men in her ringing voice. "My novices will stable and feed your horses. Your wagons will be safe here—you can unload them on the morrow. In the meantime, you must be very tired and hungry. I bid all of you come inside to eat and drink at my table and rest after your long journey."

With many sighs of relief and murmurs of, "God bless you, Milady," Arthur's men set down their gear and crowded into the house.

Mindy sat up and peered over the top railing. The place was nearly deserted. All of Morgan's helpers had gone to care for their guests.

Cautiously, she scrambled down from the cart and ran to where the horses were tethered. From one of the saddlebags, she pulled out a pair of sandals, some leggings, and a leather tunic. The sandals were too big and flopped on her feet like clown shoes, and the leggings were much too long. She tied them around her waist with a bit of twine, rolled them up around her ankles, and pulled the hood of the tunic over her hair. She now looked enough like a boy to pass undetected, assuming nobody looked too closely.

Just to make sure, Mindy scooped up some dirt and smeared it over her cheeks and forehead. Then she followed the last of Arthur's men inside. She had just congratulated herself for making it through the arched doorway unnoticed when she felt a gentle hand touch the top of her head. She froze.

"You must be Arthur's young page," said that same mellifluous voice. "I thank you for taking such good care of him. You are most welcome, lad."

Mindy didn't dare reply, so she nodded humbly and kept walking. Her eyes darted from side to side until she spotted a partially open door across the hallway, scooted inside the room, and closed the door behind her. The chamber in which she found herself was small but comfortable, with a cheery fire on the grate. She hunkered down in a shadowy corner and listened as Arthur's entourage seated themselves, joking, laughing, and thumping their tankards on the wooden serving tables.

To Mindy, they didn't sound much different than Robert and his friends having lunch in the school cafeteria; they were just louder and cruder. If they had had a burping contest, those guys would have won over Robert's soccer team, hands-down. Mindy was disappointed. She'd always pictured the Knights of the Round Table as more refined, more chivalrous, more...*knight-like.*

Someone called for music, and at the sound of a harp being tuned, the chatter and clatter of cutlery died away. A woman's voice rang out, low-pitched but true and clear. The men listened, enchanted, like obedient children.

When the very last note finally shimmered into silence, the sound of benches scraping back and Arthur's men bidding each other and their hostess good night signaled that the banquet was over.

It was a good thing too. Mindy's eyes were closed.

She was almost asleep, her head leaning against the wall, when Morgan entered. The lady crossed to the hearth and knelt on the flagstones, coaxing the dying embers back to life. When the fire was crackling to her satisfaction, she sank into a wooden chair and stretched out her legs with a contented sigh. Morgan leaned her head back, closed her eyes, and began to sing:

> "Sweet babe, a golden cradle holds thee;
> Soft a snow white fleece enfolds thee;
> Fairest flow'rs are strewn before thee;
> Sweet birds warble o'er thee:
> Shaheen, sho lo!
>
> Oh! Sleep her baby, free from sorrow,

Bright thou'lt ope thine eyes to-morrow;
Sleep while 'er thy smiling slumbers
Angels chant their numbers
Shaheen, sho lo!"

When she finished, she sat motionless, staring thoughtfully into the fire while the last note lingered in the air. Finally, she turned her head. "It is all right, lass, you can come out now."

Who, me? Mindy's mind called out.

"Yes, you. Would you like something to eat? 'Tis very late, but I am sure we could find some cold meats and mead in the pantry."

Mindy practically stopped breathing. Then before she knew it, Morgan rose, walked straight to Mindy's hiding place, and knelt down right in front of her. Even then, with her so close, it was hard to believe she was real.

Her eyes, the same pearl-grey as the mists that encircled Avalon, seemed too large for her pixie face, with its pointed chin and shining alabaster skin. It was impossible to guess her age—one moment she seemed impossibly young, the next ageless. Her feet and hands were almost as tiny as a child's.

"You cannot huddle in that corner forever, you know," she said, smiling. "Why don't you come sit by the fire and keep me company?"

"How... how did you know I was here?"

She laughed. "Oh, I felt your presence from the

moment you arrived—and I saw you sleeping from the top of the apple tree. Nothing that happens on Avalon is a secret from me, you know."

From the top of the apple tree? Then it was true what Don Lorenzo said about shape shifting. She can transform into a bird.

"Aye, a bird or a deer or a fish, or any other living creature, for that matter. There is a bit of a trick to it, but once you get the knack, 'tis really not so difficult."

Every magical being knew what Mindy was thinking before she said it. It was spooky, like there was a hidden microphone in her brain.

"But we can talk more about that later, if you'd like. At the moment, we must get you something to eat and some clean clothes. No doubt a hot bath would do as well," she added, wrinkling her nose. She pushed back Mindy's hood and took one of her braids in her hand. "Well, my young friend, it appears that you have a wee touch of the fairy blood yourself, though your technique could use some polish."

All of a sudden, the absurdity of the whole situation hit Mindy—how silly she must look in her over-sized, floppy clothes with straw in her hair and dirt all over her face. A giggle started from somewhere down in her stomach and worked its way up and out of her mouth before she could stop it.

For a moment, Morgan looked puzzled. Then she took Mindy's other braid in her hand and began to laugh too. It was such a big, hearty laugh coming from such a small person, that Mindy laughed even harder. There they were, the two of them, sitting on the floor like a couple of old friends, laughing until the tears ran down their faces.

When they finally stopped, gasping for breath, Morgan asked Mindy for her name.

"Mindy Gayle Fiddler, My Lady." She always used her full name when she wanted to impress people, and for some reason, she wanted desperately to impress this tiny, magical personage.

"Well, Miss Mindy Gayle Fiddler, I am Morgan le Fey, Lady of the Lake and Mistress of this island. But you may call me Morgan," she said, pulling Mindy to her feet. "May I call you Mindy?"

She nodded with a smile.

"Good. Come, let us see what we can find in the pantry for a hungry time-traveler."

Five minutes later, between big bites of cold meats, brown bread, and a huge piece of apple cobbler, Mindy was telling Morgan all about her mission. The food was delicious, the best she'd ever eaten, in fact, but she'd never tell Ayah, who took great pride in her cooking.

"So you see," Mindy explained, gobbling up the last of the bread, "I came to you for the magic spell. And if you don't have it, I really don't know what I'm going to do. As a matter of fact, I don't even know how to get home. Unless you can help me with that too," she finished hopefully.

Morgan thought for a moment. "You know," she said

finally, "what Don Lorenzo told you was true. I am a Druid priestess, and our magic is very ancient and very powerful. And yes, we can heal, shape shift, see the future, and many other things. But the secrets of the universe are so vast, it is not possible for any one person or teacher to possess them all, nor would it be wise. I am very sorry to disappoint you, but I do not have the spell you seek. It may very well be lost in antiquity."

"But it can't be! I can't stop Roxie without it. If she gets her computer repaired before I find the spell, she'll destroy the Internet and the world's technology. There just *has* to be someplace where the spell is written down."

"You must not lose heart, child. There is always an answer if we but have the patience and the wit to find it. I suggest," she continued, "that you talk to Arthur about your quest. He may be able to advise you further."

"Do you think so?"

"I do indeed. He is a great believer in quests, having undertaken many long and difficult ones himself. Would you like to see him?"

"Oh, yes! Right away? There's no time to lose."

"Patience, young traveler. Perhaps tomorrow. The journey from Britain has tired him greatly, and tonight he must rest. As should you—and I, for that matter. It has been a long day for all of us."

"Oh, please, I don't mean to be rude, but I need to talk with him tonight. I don't know how long I've been away, and I'm not sure how much time I have left. I don't even know what day it is."

"Travel between worlds does indeed alter one's sense of time. But I am sure there is yet time for you to complete your quest. And now," Morgan said, rising to her feet with a finality that made Mindy understand how, though she was so tiny, she exerted her authority over the inhabitants of Avalon, "the hour is late, and Arthur is long abed."

End of discussion, Mindy sighed. *Maybe it doesn't even matter. Maybe in the real world it's all over already, and I'm just wasting my time.* Mindy suddenly felt too tired to move, or care.

Unexpectedly, Morgan reached out, took her chin in her hand, and sweetly said, "Wait here," then disappeared, leaving Mindy to pick absentmindedly at the last of her supper.

Morgan reappeared so suddenly that Mindy almost knocked her drink over. "Arthur will see you now," she said, smiling. "Come quickly, we must not keep His Majesty waiting."

Before Mindy could say, "King Arthur and the Knights of the Round Table," they were knocking at a massive wooden door, and a deep voice from within was calling, "Come in."

Morgan pushed the door open, motioned Mindy inside, and retreated into the hall to give them privacy, pulling it shut behind her.

In the center of the chamber, the elaborately carved posts of a huge canopy bed on a raised platform cast long shadows across the walls and floor. A stone fireplace, tall enough for a man to stand in, emitted the only light. Three enormous mastiffs dozed fitfully on the hearth, twitching and yelping the way dogs did as they chased imaginary rabbits across the imaginary meadows in their dreams. An armored breastplate rested against a heavy oak chest at the foot of the bed.

Mindy slowly moved closer.

Arthur Pendragon, High King of Britain, Ruler of Camelot, Defender of the Faith and Protector of Avalon, lay motionless, with his eyes closed. His rugged face was as pale as the pillows beneath his head.

The bloodstained bandages wrapped about his muscular chest rose and fell with the rhythm of his labored breathing. But as Mindy approached, he opened his eyes and beckoned her closer with a bejeweled hand.

"So, my young friend," he said softly, "you are the lass my sister has been telling me about." His speech was low and resonant, somehow exactly the way Mindy expected a king's voice to sound. "You are a long way from home by the looks of you."

"Oh, yes, Your Majesty, a very long way. I came to find a magic spell to stop an evil sorceress from destroying the world I live in. I've already been to the College of Magic in Toledo, Spain with no luck, so Don Lorenzo sent me here because he said that the Lady Morgan…"

"Hold," laughed the king. "Let us begin at the beginning. What might be your name, lass?"

"Mindy, Your Majesty."

"Mindy. A lovely name, that. Now tell me, Mistress Mindy, how came you to Avalon?"

So, she told King Arthur everything from the very beginning. She gave him the details of how technology was revolutionizing the world, what she had learned from the cobra, about her encounter with Don Lorenzo Alejandro de Carpio, and her rescue by Honi the Circlemaker. Mindy finished by explaining her race against time to find the spell and use the ancient magic of the crystal ball to stop Roxanne Evillovich from using her modern magic software program in her laptop computer to cause destruction and chaos.

Arthur listened carefully, frowning from time to time, his bright blue eyes growing even brighter and his pale cheeks flushing with excitement. She had to admit, it was absolutely thrilling to have a grownup hanging on to her every word like this, especially a king! The trip to Avalon was worth the effort just for this alone.

"If all that you are telling me is true, 'tis a wonder indeed. Ah, Merlin, how I wish you were here! He predicted such marvels, you know. He told me when I was still a wee lad that someday, mankind would create wonders we have never even dreamed of—that we would fly like the birds and speak to each other over great distances as if there was no distance at all. You *have* heard of Merlin, correct?"

"Yes, Your Majesty, of course. Everybody knows about Merlin."

"Do they now? And well they should. He was my

dearest friend and teacher. He was also a great magician, perhaps the greatest who ever lived. But this thing you have told me about, this Internet—you say it can be designed any way one wants? To tell any story one wishes to tell?"

"Yes, Your Majesty, with pictures and sound and everything. You can send information anywhere in the world, and anyone with the right equipment can read it. It's just a matter of designing the website. Then people all over the world are able to read it."

The king's eyes narrowed in thought. "Could one use it, say, to tell a story about a magical kingdom that was grander, purer, stronger, and braver than any the world had ever known? Could one, for example, tell the story of Camelot, Merlin, Guinevere, and the Knights of the Round Table?"

"Oh yes, Your Majesty, absolutely. We could say anything you like—all about your court and your kingdom, and, well, everything. In fact, there are already stories about Camelot on the Internet."

"Morgan!" he shouted so unexpectedly that the dogs startled awake and began to bark and thump their heavy tails on the floor. "Morgan, come here!"

"Help me up," he commanded, struggling to rise with a grimace, and then falling back against the pillows. From the shadows behind the bed, an attendant leapt forward, but the king waved him fretfully away. When he finally spoke again, his voice was a hoarse, urgent whisper.

"I want you to do something for me lass, something

very important."

Suddenly the door of the bedchamber flew open and Morgan burst in, followed by two ladies-in-waiting. "Arthur, what is it? Are you in pain? Is the child tiring you? Shall I bring her back tomorrow?"

"Yes. No. It does not matter. I need a witness. Quickly, bring me my sword. Bring me Excalibur."

Excalibur? The Excalibur? "The sword you pulled out of the stone to become king?" Mindy exclaimed.

"The very same, lass. Come closer now, do not be shy."

Robert will go crazy when I tell him about this!

Morgan strained to unsheathe the legendary sword from its jeweled scabbard, but it was much too heavy for such a tiny person. As she struggled with the massive hilt, Mindy stepped forward and lifted the other end, and together they carried it to Arthur's side and leaned it gently upright against the bed. As soon as the king's hand fell on the shining blade, the color returned to his face and his eyes sparkled a bright, fiery blue. Energy seemed to course through his body like a lightning charge.

"Mindy, come here. My strength won't last forever, and we have no time to lose. Place your hands on Excalibur, just so. Now, repeat after me: I, Mindy of the Americas...do solemnly swear on this sword, Excalibur...that I will prevail in my noble quest against Roxanne Evillovich...and when I have finished, I will return safe and victorious to India...where I will design for Arthur Pendragon, High King of Britain...a site on the...the...what do you call it? Oh yes, the Internet...recounting the real, true, and wondrous story of the great and glorious kingdom known as Camelot...the true and valiant Knights of the Round Table...the brave and honest deeds of the aforesaid King Arthur...the beauty and charm of his legendary queen, the Lady Guinevere...the power and grace of his sister, Druid priestess, Morgan le Fey...and the wisdom of his beloved mentor, teacher, and friend, the great wizard, Merlin of Britain."

Arthur nodded, satisfied that Mindy had repeated his every word. Then, the king began sharing *his* story of Camelot with Mindy, and she hung on his every word.

He spoke of his life as a boy, his bond with Excalibur, his friendship with Merlin, his coronation as king, his marriage to Guinevere, his quests with the Knights of the Round Table, his final battle that had caused his current injuries, and his voyage to Avalon to seek Morgan's aid. As he finished, his voice began to weaken.

"There. Think you that I have forgotten anything?"

"I don't think so, Your Majesty," Mindy answered.

"Then well done! I thank you, lass, from the very bottom of my heart."

At that very moment, Excalibur's cold steel surface grew warm and bright under their hands until the entire room was bathed in its amber glow. No one moved or spoke. Even the dogs stopped whimpering. An ember crackled and broke off a log in the fire with a thump and a hiss of sparks. Outside, the stars wheeled in their constellations like sparkling diamonds in the midnight sky, and the apple blossoms wafted their sweetness into the air. The wind held its breath.

Slowly, the glow began to fade, taking Arthur's newfound strength with it. Exhausted, he fell back against the pillows and closed his eyes. A slight, weary lift of his fingers from the down coverlet signaled that the audience was at an end.

"Come," whispered Morgan, shooing Mindy gently but firmly toward the door and out into the corridor. "The king must rest."

Mindy stopped on the threshold to take one long, last look around the room. *I will never forget this moment as long as I live,* she thought. *Never, never, never.*

CHAPTER THIRTEEN

MORGAN LE FEY

The next morning dawned fair, fresh, and golden. The room in which Mindy had slept was austere and sparsely furnished, but clean and comfortable. She stretched out luxuriously and smiled to herself when she remembered the events of the night before. Then she hopped out of bed and sat down at the small oak table where a breakfast of coarse brown bread, goat cheese, fruit, and fresh spring water had been laid out.

One of Morgan's handmaidens, a tall, dark-haired girl, not much older than Mindy, clad in the simple dark blue shift of a novice, entered and curtsied.

"Good morning, Milady," she said shyly, setting down a bundle and drawing open the curtains to let in a flood of brilliant sunlight. "I have a message for you from the Lady Morgan. She is bound for Camelot in but a few hours time and is anxious to be on her way. You are to attend her as soon as you have finished your breakfast."

"Thank you. Please tell her I'll be there as soon as I'm dressed."

"I will, Milady. Shall I assist you with your hair?"

"What's your name?"

"My name is Loreena, Milady. Lady Morgan says that no one in Avalon braids as well as I."

"Yes, please, Loreena. That would be lovely."

With skillful hands, she began to brush the tangles out of Mindy's hair, twisting it expertly into two braids intertwined with bright satin ribbons. Then Loreena brought the two of them together and wrapped them like a halo around Mindy's head. All the while, she exclaimed over the color that Mindy had disliked all her life because it made her so different—and was now finally beginning to appreciate.

"The fairy folk," Loreena told her, "often have red hair. That is how you recognize them—the stronger their magic, the redder their hair—and by their small stature of course. Although, they can make themselves taller. It is most unusual," she commented, "to have a visitor from the outside world with hair so coppery-bright as yours, Milady. Do you have any fairy blood?"

Mindy thought about how her dad was always teasing her that she must have fallen off the back of a turnip truck.

"Not that I'm aware of," she laughed, "but I suppose you never know."

"Good morning," Morgan greeted Mindy warmly. "I trust you slept well?"

"Yes, quite well, thank you, Lady Morgan. How is the king?"

"Arthur is much better this morning, Goddess be praised. Your visit raised his spirits greatly."

"Oh, I'm so glad." Mindy's heart soared. To raise the spirits of one of the most famous kings who ever lived— how many people could say that?

"Come walk with me along the shore of the lake. I have urgent business outside of Avalon this day and must depart soon, but I have been thinking about your situation. There is indeed yet one more place to search for your magic spell, if you have the courage and the strength to undertake another journey. It is very far away in both time and space, but if you are willing, I will help you get there using all the magic I possess."

Another journey. This was getting a lot more complicated than Mindy had thought it would be. "Where do I have to go?"

By now, the two of them had crossed the meadow, and following a path edged with wildflowers and ferns, re-entered the thick, fragrant pine forest. Moments later, they emerged at the shore of the lake. Its bright surface sparkled in the morning sunlight. Here, Morgan paused, gazing far out across the watery surface toward the impenetrable mists that encircled the island.

"It is on the north coast of Africa," she said finally, "at a place called Alexandria. Have you ever heard of it?"

"I think so. It's Egypt now, right? My parents went there once for an engineering conference."

"Correct, but the city to which you must travel will be very different from the one your parents visited. Ancient Alexandria was not only one of the most beautiful cities ever built, it was also the undisputed mistress of the seas and a great center of intellect and culture. It was there that the Egyptian Pharaoh, Ptolemy Soter, built his great library four centuries before the birth of Christ. It is quite possible that the spell you seek may be found within the library's walls."

"An ancient library does sound like a good place to look," Mindy agreed.

"Yes, but this is no ordinary library. It was one of the wonders of antiquity, certainly the greatest before the invention of printing, and perhaps the most important collection ever. Ptolemy's dream was to gather together every book in the entire world and have them all translated into Greek—an impossible task, of course, but a noble one. It is said that every ship that entered the port of Alexandria was required to surrender all its manuscripts for the library's shelves."

"Isn't that stealing?"

"Not exactly. The manuscripts were copied by the pharaoh's scribes, and the copies were returned to the ships from whence they came. The originals were then retained in the archives."

"And you really think the magic spell might be there?"

"Well," said Morgan, plucking a black-eyed daisy and tucking it behind Mindy's ear, "Ptolemy wanted to accumulate all the wisdom and knowledge known to man. And since the ancients believed in magic, it seems only logical that the occult arts would be included in their search. Besides, at the time the library was built, there was a powerful sorceress named Agrafina living in Egypt who, before she died, wrote a compendium of everything that was then known about the Middle Realm. If you can find that manuscript, you should be able to find your spell. It seems there is no better place to look than the Library of Alexandria."

"Yes," Mindy said slowly, "I suppose you're right."

"You will make the journey, then?"

"Well..." A wave of homesickness swept over her, so strong it almost knocked Mindy off her feet. *No,* she shouted inside. *I've had enough, I want to go home!* But when she looked into Morgan's eyes, Mindy knew that it was, quite simply, too late to turn back. She had undertaken this quest because it seemed to be what she was supposed to do, although she had no idea how or why. No one had forced her to go. Besides, Mindy didn't think it made any sense to quit now that she'd come this far.

She could hear Robert's voice in her ears over and over. *"You never finish anything, never finish anything, never finish anything, never finish anything..."*

Then, there was the matter of Roxie and her magical computer program. If she got her laptop repaired before Mindy found the spell...Mindy couldn't bear to think about it.

"Yes," Mindy said, surprised at the steadiness of her voice. "I'll go."

Morgan smiled. "I was hoping you would say that. Very well then, come with me. We have work to do."

Turning away from the lake, Morgan led the way back into the forest. Mindy first thought she was retracing the path she had taken the night before, but then they turned and entered a large clearing encircled by tall oak, ash, and sycamore trees. Their leafy, lichen-covered branches met overhead, casting delicate, lacy patterns of light and shadow across the grass.

Morgan stopped, listening intently. There was no sound except the sighing of the wind through the branches and the soft rustling of leaves. "This is a holy place," she said at last. "These trees have stood here since the beginning of time. It is to this grove that the priestesses of Avalon come to be consecrated to the Goddess."

She led Mindy to the tallest tree, an enormous gnarled oak with clumps of mistletoe nestled in its lower branches.

"Give me your hands, Mindy," she commanded, pressing her palms down against the ancient bark. "Close your eyes and listen with your heart. You must clear your mind of all thought, all will, of everything except the knowledge that you are one with nature and the natural world. You are seer and soothsayer, sister to the wind, stars, and sun, and daughter of the moon, a creature of the mysteries. You have more magical power than you know. You can be whatever you wish to be, go wherever you wish to go, take whatever shape you desire. You have only to believe in yourself and whatever you seek shall be revealed to you. Do you understand?"

"Yes," Mindy whispered.

"Good. Now listen and tell me what you hear."

"I...I don't hear anything."

"Try harder. Concentrate. Use your power."

Mindy shut her eyes tightly, so tight that even the dancing patterns of light and shadow beneath her eyelids disappeared. But the only thing she could hear was her own heart pounding like a jackhammer.

She took a deep breath to quiet it, then another, and another. And finally, slowly, ever so slowly, Mindy became aware of another heartbeat, surer and steadier than her own, barely audible at first, then growing stronger and stronger, until it drowned out everything but the sound of Morgan's voice.

The pounding made Mindy dizzy, and she wrapped her arms around the tree trunk to steady herself. A rhythmic *kathump, kathump, kathump* vibrated through her whole body, from the top of her head to the tips of her toes. It came from nowhere and everywhere all at once, and when Morgan spoke again, her voice seemed to come from very far away. "What do you hear, Mindy?"

"I hear...a heartbeat, like...like...I can't describe it. It's almost as if it's coming from inside the tree. I can hear it, but I can feel it, too."

"Good. Match your breathing to its pace. Become one with its rhythm."

Mindy pressed her cheek against the bark, breathing in its rich, earthy scent. Morgan's voice broke through the wall of sound softly at first, then gradually louder. The familiar words sent a shock wave through every nerve in Mindy's body.

"Maker of the universe," Morgan intoned, "you who hears all, sees all, and knows all, hear my plea. Remove this young seeker from the holy Isle of Avalon and transport her to the city of Alexandria in the days of its greatest glory so that she may complete her quest and return home safely to her family. Maker of the universe, I will not move from this sacred grove until you have shown mercy to your petitioner. Spirit of the earth, *hear my plea!* Spirit of the sky, *hear my plea!* Goddess of the Middle Realm and all that dwells within and between—HEAR MY PLEA!"

As the words echoed and died away, the forest sounds receded into the distance, and a strange tingling lightness swept over Mindy. The tree trunk melted slowly away at the same time as the earth fell from beneath her feet—but not before a strong wind surrounded her, lifting her up, light as a feather, rushing past her face, cool, then warm, then cool again. Weightless, bodiless, Mindy floated somewhere out of time and place, suspended languidly between worlds, eyes closed, drifting as easily as a cloud.

A gust of salt-sea air drenched in sunlight and seaweed hit Mindy with such force that her eyes flew open. Far below, white flecks of foam tossed and danced on the waves of an endless expanse of water that varied from a deep indigo blue to a shimmering turquoise. Seabirds skimmed the surface, dove for fish, and reappeared with bright flashes of silver in their beaks. Sprawling beds of lacy brown kelp floated lazily up and down in the swells.

Mindy was so startled at the realization that she was suspended in mid-air, that she lost her concentration and then her balance, and before she knew it, she was plunging downward like a kite in a tailspin. Instinctively, she lifted her head and spread her arms wide, and as she did so, she saw not arms and hands, but wings and feather tips. Mindy had magically transformed into a seagull.

The wind buoyed her up, sending her effortlessly skyward again. It was wonderful, more wonderful than anything Mindy had ever known—this near weightlessness—the most wonderful sensation in the world. When she turned her head from side to side, she could see for miles in every direction.

She tilted this way and that, getting used to her new body. As her confidence grew, she practiced turns, hurtling toward the wave tops at lightning speed, banking sharply and spiraling upward again in giddy curves, like a giant roller coaster, only a hundred thousand times better. When Mindy began to tire, she simply stretched her wings out and let the wind do the work.

She had been flying for several hours before she spotted a dark line on the horizon—land! Gradually, the line became a wave-washed coast, the sea-swells gave way to an ocean of glittering sand, and moments later, Mindy was soaring high above the dunes of the Arabian Desert. The cool ocean air currents gave way to rising, rippling waves of heat. Only a few lonely caravans wending their way slowly across the dunes broke the monotony of the barren landscape.

Later in the day, Mindy spotted the green fringe of an oasis. A dozen complaining camels and their drivers rested in the welcome shade of a few dilapidated date palms. She flapped down and helped herself to a few plump dates from right under their noses. They completely ignored her. Then she hopped to the water's edge. The pool looked cool and inviting.

After a few moments of splashing and tossing flecks of water into the air with her beak, and some sips of the fresh water, Mindy was on her way, letting her instincts guide her. They seemed to know where she was headed, even if she didn't have a clue.

The sun was just beginning its descent in the sky when she reached the western shoreline of the Arabian Peninsula with its sun-baked villages. Mindy veered northward over the Sea of Reeds, lavender in the setting sun, and sailed serenely out over the dark turquoise waters of the Mediterranean.

Completely accustomed to her new form, Mindy had been gliding effortlessly for hours, so close to the water that she could almost graze the surface with her wingtips. But she was beginning to tire, and there was no land in sight. She had to find someplace to rest soon.

PART FOUR:

ALEXANDRIA, EGYPT

1ST CENTURY B.C.

CHAPTER FOURTEEN

ZENODOTUS

As the Greek merchant ship *Aphrodite* made her way across the open sea, Zeno laid aside his manuscript with a sigh and sat back against the cushions, listening to the rhythmic creaking of the ship's timbers. Snug and solitary in his hammock in the *Aphrodite's* forward quarters, he had been reading all morning and well into the afternoon. Only now that the sun was going down did he remember that he had not eaten since breakfast.

He swung his long legs over the side of the hammock, stretched out his lanky frame, and went up on deck. It was stuffy below, and as he took in deep gulps of fresh, salt-sea air, he realized how hungry he was. Zeno was a studious, good-natured lad of fourteen. From his father, he had inherited his penchant for learning and an almost obsessive love of books, the legacy of his famous ancestor, Greek scholar, politician, and orator, Demetrius of Phalaron.

Demetrius had earned his fame and fortune at the court of Ptolemy I. Together the two men had amassed the greatest collection of books in the ancient world and hired resident scholars to painstakingly translate them all into Greek. Demetrius was a man of the world. As the Master of the Library, and the king's close friend and advisor, he lived a life of luxury, power, and privilege—at least while his patron was alive.

Over two centuries later, his great, great, great—well, he wasn't exactly sure how many greats, but certainly a great many—grandson, Zenodotus, or Zeno as his family called him, was returning to his duties as assistant to the present-day Master of the Keepers of the Books.

Someday when his apprenticeship was finished, Zeno would assume responsibility for the vast collection of knowledge and the small army of slaves, scribes, and translators that maintained it. It was a prospect that he looked forward to with great anticipation. Indeed, once he assumed his full duties, he would be one of the most important and powerful personages in all of Alexandria.

Zeno loved the library and its cool, elegant, marbled corridors and endless shelves filled with manuscripts, with all his heart. In fact, he spent almost all of his time within its hushed confines, undoubtedly more than was good for him.

At the beginning of the third year of his apprenticeship, his superiors, noting his pallor and lack of interest in any of the things in which young men of fourteen usually took an interest, had sent him off on a voyage to Greece.

"All things in moderation," they'd told him. "You are working too hard. Visit the Acropolis. Swim in the sea, lie in the sun, meet some young ladies, write some poetry. Take a few months away from the library—the change will do you good."

So Zeno had reluctantly packed his few belongings and some books and sailed off to visit his family in Athens with no thought but to count the days until his return.

Once he'd arrived, he was glad he'd made the voyage. It had been good to see his brothers and sisters again after such a long time away, good to be out in the bright sunshine, free, for once, of lessons, manuscripts, and responsibilities.

Sitting beneath the olive tree on the terrace of his parents' villa overlooking the sea, Zeno had savored freshly baked bread and country cheese and pondered at length the philosophy his teachers had impressed upon him since he was a small boy:

"From careful observation of the reality of things, and the systematic inquiry into the origins and experiences of life, we should know ourselves and to ourselves be true— pursuing the good and beautiful, and rejecting that which is evil and imperfect."

Zeno had turned the matter over in his mind. His was not a rebellious nature, and he had no reason to doubt his teachers. But the truth was, that in his brief and sheltered life, he'd had very little experience with the world. The very idea that there might be other realms beyond his knowledge—which were fantastic, unpredictable, and filled with turmoil, wickedness, and excess—had lately begun to both disturb and intrigue him.

The library, and the self-contained complex that surrounded it, was a world unto itself, a safe haven of beauty, richness, quiet, and pleasure. Surely it was all that he could ever want or need. *And yet...there must be more!* he'd thought.

Now he was on his way back to his beloved library and his well-ordered existence, and as much as he looked forward to resuming his duties, he felt unaccountably restless. In short, without being able to put a face or name to his longings, Zeno hungered for adventure.

He was making his way toward the bow when he spotted a lone seagull circling overhead. The seagull then dove straight for the ship and tottered to a landing on the wooden crossbar halfway down the mainmast.

A moment later when Zeno looked up again, instead of the seagull, he was astonished to see a girl, not much younger than himself, clinging improbably to the mainmast. He had no idea there *were* any girls on board, let alone one brave enough to climb the rigging.

"Hello," he shouted. "Are you looking for the seagull?"

For a moment, Mindy was completely confused. She couldn't think of an answer.

"The one that just...say, are you all right up there?"

"I...I think so. I'm just not quite sure how to get down."

"Oh, that is easy. Work your way over to the rigging and climb down the rope ladder—over there on the left. Do you see it?"

She could see it all right, but it looked awfully high off the deck. Besides, she was still in shock at finding herself in human form again. Things seemed to happen so suddenly.

"I don't know if I can get to it."

"Do not worry, take your time. When you get to the bottom rung, you can just swing out over the deck and jump. I will catch you."

Yeah, right. Maybe he thought he was strong enough to catch someone her size, but he didn't look very sturdy to Mindy. Unfortunately, there didn't seem to be much choice.

Hand over hand, she inched her way onto the rigging, hanging on for dear life, because the ship was plunging up and down in the swells like a bucking bronco.

Finally, she reached the heavy rope ladder and climbed down until she was standing on the bottom rung. The boy was squinting up at her, shading his eyes against the sun.

"Are you sure you can catch me?"

"Sure," he said cheerfully. "I am stronger than I look. I work at a library. I carry heavy books around all day."

"You mean *the* library? The Library of Alexandria? You actually *work* there?"

"Yes. If you come down, I will tell you all about it."

"Okay," she said hesitantly. *Don't think about it, just do it.* Mindy closed her eyes, took a deep breath, and hurled out into space. She landed right on top of the poor guy, and the next thing she knew, they were on the deck in a jumbled heap. He sat up laughing and extended his hand to pull her to her feet.

"Nice jump," he said. "My name is Zenodotus. My friends call me Zeno."

"Mindy," she offered, dusting herself off with one hand and shaking his with the other. "Thanks for your help."

That's when it happened. Mindy stood there, frozen, staring at him. All she could think of was how kind his eyes were, and what a nice mouth he had, and how there was a dimple in his left check when he smiled, and...

"I did not think there were any girls on this ship," Zeno said finally, blushing and letting go of her hand. "What were you doing up there?"

"Up there? Oh, well, I was just...um...I mean..." Even Mindy couldn't think of a way to explain this one. Better to tell the truth and hope he wouldn't think she was completely crazy.

"Can you keep a secret?" she asked, lowering her voice to a whisper.

"Of course."

"You know that seagull that was here a few minutes ago? It was really me...I can shape shift. But I didn't do it all by myself—I had help from a Druid priestess on the Isle of Avalon so I could get to the Library of Alexandria to look for a magic spell..." Mindy stopped. How could she possibly make someone from this time understand the reason for her mission?

Zeno frowned. "Go on."

"It's very difficult to explain."

"Perhaps you should start over again from the very beginning. You talk awfully fast, and you have an unusual accent. I am not quite used to the sound of it yet."

Suddenly, the bell from the crow's nest high above their heads began to clang violently. "The lighthouse!" shouted the lookout in a deep, booming voice. "Increase oars!"

"INCREASE OARS!" repeated the quartermaster. The *Aphrodite* sprang forward.

"The Lighthouse! Mindy, look! There—that bright light on the horizon. That is Pharos Island. It stands at the mouth of the Alexandria Harbor to guide the ships in. You can see its beacon from twenty-five miles out to sea. That means we will be home by tomorrow morning!"

Mindy turned and saw a distant point of light burning clear and steadfast across the darkened water. "Thank goodness. To tell you the truth, I'm a little anxious to get this over with and go home. I'm sure everyone must be terribly worried about me by now."

"Do not distress, I know my way around the library better than anybody. If you tell me exactly what it is you are looking for, I can almost certainly help you find it."

They hunkered back down in the bow beside the heavy coiled rope, sheltered from the wind. As the *Aphrodite* moved through the night swells, Mindy told Zeno the whole story, every word, from the very beginning.

She figured he'd pretty much write her off as crazy, but he listened carefully to every word and only stopped her once or twice to ask questions. She'd never talked to anyone like this, as if she'd known him her whole life and still couldn't get words out fast enough. The stars were just beginning to fade when they finally fell asleep holding each other's hands.

Mindy awoke to the breaking of waves against the prow. The *Aphrodite* was slicing briskly through the aqua waters like a pony hurrying toward the stables after a long ride, as if it sensed it was almost home. The sky was a quiet seashell pink, and the sails, which had been unfurled to their fullest to catch the wind, glowed tangerine in the sunrise.

For a moment, Mindy forgot where she was. She yawned and stretched, feeling the morning chill and a cramp in her muscles. Beside her, Zeno still slept curled up peacefully against the ropes. Mindy got up as gently as she could so as not to wake him and walked to the railing.

There! Looming straight ahead on the horizon, the slim, elegant column of the Pharos Lighthouse rose in all its splendor. As the sun climbed higher, the polished marble facade turned from soft rose to a blinding white. The torchlight from the night before had been replaced with a thick column of grey smoke that curled upward into the morning sky.

The lighthouse was the marvel of the age. Its four tiers, with their intricate maze of stairways, passages, and apartments, rose four hundred feet into the air. At the top of the third tier, in an open space surrounded by eight marble columns capped with a domed top, a huge fire burned continuously. Its light beamed far out to sea by the use of huge reflectors. From atop the dome, a twenty-foot bronze statue of Poseidon, half man and half fish, both loved and feared, leaned on his trident surveying the panorama below.

Zeno joined her at the railing, awakened by the hustle and bustle on deck as the crew prepared to dock. The *Aphrodite* corrected her course and veered to the southeast, heading for the mouth of the harbor. As they streamed majestically past the lighthouse, Zeno read aloud the inscription in large Greek letters at the base:

SOSTRATUS THE CNIDIAN,
SON OF DEXJFANOS, DEDICATES THIS
TO THE SAVIOR GODS ON BEHALF
OF THOSE WHO SAIL THE SEAS.

To the east, directly across from Pharos Island and almost touching it, another long, slender arm of land curved out to encircle the harbor in a protective embrace, forming the narrow straits through which they passed over the reef into the Eastern Harbor.

The royal palaces of the city's ruling kings and queens rose upon this second arm of land, connected to the adjoining buildings by a wide avenue lined with colonnades of rare Egyptian marble. Within these walls, the descendants of Alexander the Great, conqueror of the greatest empire the world had ever known, lived in unimaginable splendor.

The extraordinary beauty of Alexandria was, without question, unequaled anywhere in the ancient world. Its elegant marble buildings, magnificent public squares, and broad vistas lined with statuary rivaled even those of Rome. There were theaters, wild animal parks, temples to a vast pantheon of gods, particularly Greek and Egyptian, gardens of tropical plants—and the Library of Alexandria.

Visitors approaching the city by land entered and departed through two huge archways, the Sun Gate to the north and the Moon Gate to the south. The Royal Greek Macedonian quarter with its palaces, government offices, and marts of trade occupied the entire front of the Great Harbor. Here stood the stately mausoleum where Alexander was buried, swathed in the finest linen and bound in plates of gold.

Directly south stretched the native Egyptian quarter where the common laborers lived. To the east, almost as large as the Greek quarter, the city's Jewish population dwelt within its own walls—a city within a city.

The *Aphrodite* dropped anchor at the base of the broad marble steps that ascended from the transparent turquoise waters of the port to the thoroughfares leading into the city.

Mindy took a deep breath. She couldn't believe she was really about to set foot in such a fascinating, ancient, and famous city. Then she felt a pit of nervousness in her stomach. Would it be dangerous in such an enormous and expansive city? Would she be able to find the spell? What if it wasn't in the library after all?

Stop it, she chided herself. *I have to be brave. I have all the power I need to get me through this adventure, as long as I believe in myself.*

She took another deep breath. It was time. Mindy glanced at Zeno, and he gave her a reassuring smile.

"Ready?" he asked.

No turning back now, Mindy thought. "Yes, ready as I'll ever be."

Zeno took her hand, and together they disembarked the *Aphrodite.*

CHAPTER FIFTEEN

THE LIBRARY

Everywhere, the atmosphere of Alexandria was bustling and festive. As Mindy and Zeno made their way along the broad avenue that skirted the waterfront, she thought that never, not even in India, had she seen so many different kinds of people.

Swarthy Greeks mingled with Arabians in flowing robes. Exquisitely coiffed Babylonians in brightly colored turbans, rubbed shoulders with war-like Gauls and elegant Iberians.

Macedonian soldiers pushed their way through the crowds, swaggering arrogantly in their short-skirted uniforms of finely tooled leather with stout swords buckled to their sides.

Wealthy Egyptian women peeked through the draperies of their litters and wrinkled their noses in disdain as they shouted orders to their slaves.

Mindy realized these poor, wretched souls must have been captured from distant lands and sold into servitude, most likely never to see their homes or families again. In Alexandria, Zeno told her, human beings were bought and sold in the local bazaar for less than the cost of a good horse or a well-crafted urn. Mindy was about to ask where the slave market was when she noticed the rose petals under their feet and the garlands draped along both sides of the corniche leading toward the royal palaces.

"For Caesar," Zeno explained as they passed between marble columns entwined with marigolds. "He arrived a few days ago with thirty-two hundred legionaries and eight hundred horses. There is a royal banquet tonight in his honor. The queen wants to impress him."

"Which queen?" she asked.

"Cleopatra, of course. Caesar is here to settle a dispute between her and her brother, King Ptolemy. He is also her husband, by the way—a mere formality," he added hastily. "It is the custom here. He is only ten years old. That is why he has three advisors to rule the country for him."

Wow! Mindy thought. *Cleopatra—one of the most famous women in history. I wish I could meet her! I wonder if there is a way, even just to see her...*

"Anyway," Zeno continued, breaking Mindy's train of thought, "since her father died, Cleopatra has wanted to rule Egypt herself. But when the king's advisors drove her out, she went to Syria and raised an army to come back and fight for the throne. Her troops are waiting at the border.

"Caesar invited her to Alexandria to sign a truce. But, I heard that the young king's advisors surrounded the palace with soldiers and ordered them to kill the queen on sight if she tried to get in. It is funny if you think about it—three big, powerful men, afraid of one twenty-year-old woman.

"However, Cleopatra is no ordinary woman. Her servants carried her into the palace wrapped up in a carpet. When they unrolled it in Caesar's study, she fell right out onto the floor at his feet and started speaking to him in perfect Latin. Of course, he fell madly in love with her. At least that is the story I heard as we landed. It is the talk of the town."

"Do you think we'll be able to get into the library with all the commotion?" Mindy queried.

"Of course. Actually, our timing could not be better. My master will be at the banquet. He is to take Caesar on a tour of the library after dinner. That is part of the job I will do someday—entertaining visiting dignitaries," he added with pride. "Everyone will be busy with the preparations. They will not even notice us. By the way, Caesar is a great lover of books."

"I thought he was a general."

"He is, but he is a scholar too, and for good reason."

"How does he have time to read when he has a whole empire to run?"

"That is the whole point. You know that Alexander the Great created the biggest empire the world has even seen?"

"So?"

"So, all the people he conquered speak different languages and have different customs and religions. When King Ptolemy inherited Alexander's kingdom, he realized that in order to rule so many people, he had to understand them, and to understand them, he had to study them. That's why he collected their books and brought learned men from every corner of the empire to translate the manuscripts into Greek. His advisors read them and kept him informed about what his subjects were up to."

"Oh, I see. What a brilliant idea."

"Yes, I agree. And royal libraries were built in all the Hellenistic capitals, not just to impress people, but to rule them. That is why the Library of Alexandria is so important. It is the greatest collection of books and scholars in history. Someday, by the time I am Master of the Keepers of the Books, we will have a copy of every single manuscript in the whole world!" Zeno paused, noticing Mindy's face. "What is the matter?"

"If there are so many books, how can we possibly find one magic spell? It could be anywhere in the library."

"Not so. Everything is placed by category, and within each category there are divisions and subdivisions arranged alphabetically by the author's name."

"Is there a section on magic?"

"Oh yes, quite a large one, although not as extensive as some of the others. Do not worry. It may take a little time, but we will find it. How long are you planning to stay?"

"That's the problem. I wasn't planning to stay at all. My family doesn't know where I am. They must be frantic by now."

"Well then, we will have to find a magic spell to make time stand still so that when you get home, they will never even know you left."

Was he teasing her? She couldn't be sure. "Is there such a thing?"

"I do not know, but it is certainly worth a try. Ah, here we are!" Zeno exclaimed.

They had arrived at the royal complex. It was flanked on one side by acres of elegant parks and lush, carefully tended gardens. On the other side was the royal harbor where an extravagant, floating pleasure palace—the queen's private barge—basked peacefully in the sun. The balconies of Cleopatra's palace were adorned with brilliantly colored flags that fluttered in the breeze from the bay.

"Where is the library?" Mindy whispered.

"Inside the museum. You will see."

They marched up a long avenue lined with palm trees and alabaster sphinxes, cat-like creatures the height of twenty men with a woman's head and the body of a lion. As they neared the carved bronze doors, the palace guards— tall, muscular Nubians with impassive faces and glistening black skin—sprang forward and crossed their spears to block their way.

When they recognized Zeno, they instantly sprang

back again. The two of them then passed unimpeded from the hot, glaring sunlight into the cool interior. Mindy looked at Zeno with awe.

"It is only because I have been around here since I was a little boy," Zeno explained, blushing. "They all know me. I am still just myself."

But Mindy could tell that he was secretly pleased.

To hide his embarrassment, Zeno turned and led the way from the cavernous entry hall through an endless maze of rooms, courtyards, and galleries. Mindy and Zeno passed cloisters, refectories, sleeping apartments, and common areas. This was where hundreds of royal scholars passed their days free of worries or taxes, contemplating the history of the world, uncovering the secrets of nature, and making lasting contributions to science.

Everywhere she looked, the walls were covered with brilliantly painted bas-reliefs. The ceilings were a deep blue, studded with glittering stars, and the floors were made of richly veined marble, cool and smooth as glass.

In her mind, Mindy tried to retrace the course they had taken, but she had lost all sense of direction. "This place is a rat's maze," she said, trying to sound lighthearted. "How are we going to get out of here?"

Zeno laughed. "Do not worry, I can find my way around with my eyes closed. Besides, this place is supposed to be a labyrinth. One of its most important functions is to conceal the location where Ramses is buried."

"You mean one of the pharaohs' mummies is in here?"

"Yes, we have to pass under the tomb to reach the library. We are almost there."

Moments later, they arrived at the entrance to Alexander's tomb. Sacred images of ancient Egypt adorned every wall. There were snow-white ibis with dark-tipped, iridescent plumage, crocodiles with gaping jaws and cruel teeth, elegant fan-tailed falcons, the sacred ram with its downward-curving horns, and the Apis bull with the sun disk on its head. Their onyx eyes followed Mindy and Zeno as they moved from room to room.

At last they emerged at Alexander's tomb. The sarcophagus stood within a gold circle almost seven hundred feet long. It was surrounded by inlaid images of the astrological signs in grass-green malachite veined with deep emerald, royal blue lapis, amber tiger's eye, glossy black marble, rusty red carnelian, and pale pink quartz.

Zeno and Mindy skirted the tomb as quickly as they could, so as not to disturb the spirits of the dead, and entered the broad marble colonnade that connected the museum with the neighboring building. Thoth, the god of knowledge, and his sister, Seshat, patroness of archives, stood solemn guard at the entryway.

Mindy read aloud the words etched in the stone: "THE PLACE OF THE CURE OF THE SOUL."

"What a strange name," she whispered. Then she realized that she could not only speak and understand the languages of whatever place she visited on her quest, but could also read them. Once again she thought to herself.

Thanks, Agamede.

Here, too, were sculpted images of the pantheon of Egyptian deities: Osiris, god of fertility; Seth and Isis, god of the desert and his beloved queen; Amun-Re, the lord of the sun; Anubis, the jackal-headed god of the underworld; Nut, the sky-goddess; the earth-god, Geb; Horus, the falcon-god; Heh, the lord of infinity; and Sekhment, the lion-headed goddess of war and her husband, Ptah, god of craftsmen and architects.

At the threshold, Zeno paused. Within this roofed passageway was the world's greatest collection of scrolls and manuscripts, the fabulous Library of Alexandria.

Nearly three-quarters of a million books, carefully translated and lovingly categorized, were arranged along its walls on shelves of perfumed cedar, richly textured mahogany, and fine-grained myrtlewood. The shelves rose tier upon tier to the shadowy ceiling. Here and there, a brightly colored ribbon hung down to show that something had been removed.

Just as Zeno had described, each niche was devoted to a different category. In front of every section stood a wooden stand holding a massive papyrus ledger into which every borrowed manuscript was faithfully recorded to ensure that nothing was lost or stolen.

A long row of study tables down the center of the colonnade provided a working place for the scholars, but the library was silent and deserted. Everyone was preparing for the evening's celebration. Cleopatra's entertainments were legendary—no trouble or expense was spared.

To Mindy's dazzled eyes, the Library of Alexandria was as vast and mysterious as the Toledo Cathedral. There were more books than she had ever dreamed existed.

Zeno led her quickly to the shelves where the manuscripts about magic and the occult were kept. "See?" he said. "I told you it was smaller than the other sections."

"I guess it depends on what you call 'smaller,'" she laughed. "It still looks like an awful lot of books to me...We need to look for a manuscript by Agrafina," Mindy added, recalling the name Morgan had given her. "She wrote the book that should have the magic spell I need in it. At least we don't have to go any further than the A's."

"Great! Let us get started. Here, you take this side, I will start at the other end, and we will meet in the middle and work our way up."

"Good idea!"

One by one, they began pulling down the manuscripts and rolling them out, some old and fragile, others crisp and new. Out of the corner of her eye, Mindy noted how Zeno handled each one with infinite care, running his fingers tenderly over the smooth pages as if he were stroking the cheek of a newborn baby.

It had seemed a reasonable task, going through the A's, but by late afternoon they were still empty-handed. Mindy had just prepared to close another manuscript and return it to its proper place on the shelf, when her eyes fell on a caption midway down a page. "Circlemaking: A Guide to the Creation and Use of Circles for Travel Through Time and Space," she translated.

Mindy's heart leapt into her throat. There it was—a perfectly rendered drawing of a circle divided into ten equal sections, each marked with a symbol, just as Honi had drawn them in the Cathedral of Toledo. Beneath the picture, a brief paragraph instructed the reader which incantation to recite at the completion of each section. This was more than a spell—it was her ticket home.

She looked around. She could copy a page from one of the papyrus ledgers, but there were no pens in sight and not enough time. Mindy closed her eyes and tried to memorize the page, but the images spun in her mind and refused to stay still.

She watched Zeno out of the comer of her eye, and when Mindy was sure he was too absorbed in what he was reading to notice, she carefully tore the page out. She felt like a thief—no, worse. Removing a page from a book wasn't theft, it was sacrilege—a crime against nature and humanity, punishable by banishment from every library on the face of the earth from now until the end of time.

Still, Mindy thought, desperate times called for desperate measures. She folded the page into little squares and tucked it carefully into her pocket so he would not see what she had done to the precious manuscript.

Zeno looked up at her and smiled. "Is everything all right?"

"Fine," she said. "Have you found anything?"

"Not yet," he answered cheerfully, "but we must be getting closer."

In their combined effort, they had searched all the bottom tiers and had to climb the ladders to retrieve more manuscripts. In the waning light, the titles were becoming harder and harder to read.

Mindy squinted across another row: Adamentis, Agememnon, Agesilaus, Agrafina, Agrafma, Arsenius...?

"This is it!" she cried, almost falling off the ladder. "This is the one! Come on, help me get it down."

Together they lowered the cumbersome manuscript off the shelf and onto the nearest table. "We had better hurry," Zeno muttered. "The guards will be here any minute to light the torches."

"Okay, okay, I'm hurrying."

"Why don't you stand by the door and signal when the royal tour is coming while I copy the pages?"

"It's a deal." Mindy sprinted down the length of the passageway as fast as she could and stationed herself between Thoth and Seshat so that she could see in both directions. Her thoughts were whirling like they had been at the Toledo Cathedral.

Once the spell was in her hands, she could draw herself a circle and get home in no time, which really cheered her up—until it hit her. If she returned to India, she would never see Zeno again, and she was really starting to like him. *You came here to accomplish something*, she reminded herself, *and now you've done it. It's a small price to pay for saving the whole world. Nobody said this was going to be easy.* But, then she remembered Zeno's gentle smile and felt a funny little tug on her heart.

Suddenly, a gleam of torchlight glanced off the chamber walls, and then Mindy heard voices and approaching footsteps. She hurried back to the Magic and Occult section. "There's somebody coming. Did you find it?"

Zeno didn't answer her question. "Here," he said, shoving the manuscript into her arms. "Put this back. I will greet them and make up some excuse about why we are here. I am not expected back at work until tomorrow. We do not want to arouse suspicion."

"But did you find the spell?"

"Later. We do not have much time."

"Wait a minute, you can't...Zeno, come back!"

But he was already gone, walking with calm dignity toward the crowd that had gathered at the entrance while servants placed flaming torches into the sconces along the library walls. Soon the hall was aglow with light.

CHAPTER SIXTEEN

CLEOPATRA

The entourage approached Mindy slowly, led by Zeno. He was engaged in animated conversation with a tall, silver-haired man of powerful military bearing who must have been Caesar, and an elegantly clad woman, who by her royal bearing, could only be the legendary Cleopatra, Queen of the Nile, Ruler of Upper and Lower Egypt.

Behind them, flanked by the highest ranks of the library staff, came a gaggle of courtiers, noblemen, and scholars attended on all sides by slaves brandishing peacock feather fans. Everyone appeared to be in fine spirits, especially Caesar.

For someone of his day and age, the powerful statesman and Roman general was considered advanced in years. Yet at fifty-two, Caesar did not look old, particularly on this day. He was still in excellent form; athletic, graceful, and handsome, even if he was slightly bald. Indeed, his wife had hoped that her husband's thinning hair would make him less attractive to other women.

But alas, he was not only one of the richest and most powerful men in the ancient world, he was also one of the most charming. His baldness notwithstanding, women found him quite irresistible.

Caesar's manners were impeccable, his habits moderate, and his personality both intense and compelling. His was a life of political intrigue, military peril, and domestic scandal, yet he still found time to indulge his passion for knowledge with the eager enthusiasm of youth. He found the young Egyptian queen, with her keen mind, subtle wit, and flair for languages, the most captivating woman he had ever met—which was, of course, exactly what she wanted him to think.

At the time she was unceremoniously unrolled onto the floor of Caesar's chamber, Cleopatra was at the height of her beauty. Her indomitable lust for life, uncanny comprehension of politics and court intrigue, and ambition, were carefully concealed beneath a manner at once stately and feminine. She was a small, highly intelligent woman of Macedonian-Greek blood—brilliant, well educated, knowledgeable, and poised far beyond her years.

The outline of her figure, visible through the fine, diaphanous linen of her gown, suggested a goddess-like perfection of form. Yet, she was not beautiful in the classic sense. Her nose was too large and her mouth too wide to inspire the praise of poets. Instead, Cleopatra beguiled with her voice, which was as low and resonant as a finely tuned musical instrument. She had turned all her charms upon her esteemed guest, delighting him with her spirit and astonishing him with an intellect that was thought of as rare for a woman of her time. As was to be expected, the mighty Caesar was utterly captivated.

He had just spent an enchanting morning touring the sites of Alexandria with the queen as his guide. Together they had visited the city's theaters, zoos, and parks, and admired the architectural splendor of its towering obelisks and monuments. They knelt in solemn reverence at the tomb of the divine Alexander. They inspected the royal granaries, toured the vast palaces of the Ptolemaic kings, and then, for the final crowning glory, climbed to the very top of the Pharos Lighthouse and gazed across the sparkling, sun-drenched harbor to the open sea.

As the royal chariot carried them back down the Great Boulevard that divided the city into north and south, Caesar had admitted to himself that the wonders of Alexandria surpassed any city in the empire—even imperial Rome.

They had arrived at the palace in the early afternoon for a light but sumptuous lunch, and before the evening's festivities, Caesar had requested a tour of the famous library. Thus it was that Mindy now found herself frozen to her spot, as two of the most powerful people in the ancient world strolled toward her with Zeno between them.

Zeno's face was glowing with pride. Here in the place

he knew and loved best in all the world, he was poised and completely self-assured.

Mindy's heart sank, however, every time he looked at the queen. Clearly Cleopatra was very charming. Mindy watched as Zeno bent down and whispered into the royal ear as if they had been the best of friends for years. The queen's warm, throaty laughter filled the hall.

The entourage halted directly in front of Mindy. Fans fluttered. Dozens of haughty, kohl-lined eyes turned in her direction. She could feel the blood pounding in her cheeks. To hide her confusion, she sank into a deep curtsy.

"Your Eminences," Zeno pronounced, "may I present my cousin, the Lady Mindora of Phaleron. She is visiting our city from the Greek Islands and expressed a desire to visit the Royal Library. Her father is a great scholar and translator of texts."

"Arise, my child. You are welcome to Alexandria," said the queen in her melodious voice.

Zeno stepped to Mindy's side and brought her to her feet with a warm, strong hand cupped beneath her elbow.

When Mindy looked up, the queen's huge, dark eyes were watching her with amusement. To her utter astonishment, Cleopatra's hair shone like rich, burnished copper in the amber torchlight. *Wow, she's a redhead...just like me.*

"I was just explaining to my cousin the organization of the books and how they are acquired and translated," Zeno clarified.

"Are you interested in scholarly pursuits, Lady Mindora?" inquired Caesar in his abrupt, yet kindly manner. "That is most unusual for a young woman—except for present company, of course," he added, nodding to Cleopatra.

"Oh yes, sir, I love to read," Mindy replied. "I get a lot of books from the Internet...ouch!" Zeno gave her elbow a sharp warning pinch.

"I beg your pardon," said Caesar. "There seems to be an echo. What was that you said?"

"She said, Great Caesar, that books are like *a net*. One gets caught up in them so easily."

Nice cover-up, Zeno! Mindy noted to herself.

"Ah yes, one does indeed. Well then, Master Zenodotus, if Lady Mindora will be so kind as to indulge an old man's fancy," nodding to Mindy with a twinkle in his eye, "may I suggest that you begin your tour from the beginning, so you may inform us all about the workings of this marvelous library of yours? Tell me, how many volumes did you say have been collected here?"

"Nearly three-quarters of a million, Great Caesar. Actually, there are two libraries—this one and a smaller one in the Egyptian quarter. The main library contains some five hundred thousand volumes, and the smaller, let me see, a third again more. That makes a total of over seven hundred thousand manuscripts altogether, I believe—the greatest collection of Hellenic literature in the world."

"Remarkable, quite remarkable! Do you have other

writings as well?"

"Oh yes, we have translations of the most important works of theology, history, art, medicine, philosophy, and science, from Egypt, Babylonia, Assyria, Phoenicia, Syria, Persia, Ethiopia, and India. We even have the books of the Hebrews, translated into Greek, of course.

"Seventy-two scholars, six from each of the twelve tribes of Israel, were brought from the Holy City of Jerusalem and locked up in the lighthouse from morning till night, until their task was completed. If Caesar would like to see the translations, they are at your disposal."

"Like to see them? Of course I would like to see them!" Caesar paused before one of the polished shelves and peered at the titles. "And what have we here?"

"This is the beginning of the Science section. As you can see, we have divided the main room into ten large sections, with smaller separate chambers for special study and lectures."

As they continued down the length of the hall, Zeno explained the contents of each section, stopping now and then to offer an amusing anecdote about the acquisition of a particular book. The more Zeno spoke, the more excited Caesar became.

From time to time, he paused to command that a particular scroll be unrolled for his inspection. Soon, the tables in the center of the room were littered with manuscripts.

"We also offer classes and readings of the classic

poets," Zeno concluded as the group made its way back to the Magic section. "Perhaps Caesar would like to be entertained with a poetry reading after dinner?"

"That would be spectacular. Cleopatra?"

"Yes, Great Caesar," she said.

"I must say, this is absolutely fantastic, far beyond my wildest imagination. I had heard about this library, but to see with my own eyes, how extensive it is—I am genuinely awestruck. You have done a magnificent job, my dear, absolutely splendid!" he added, turning to Cleopatra. Then Caesar addressed Zeno once again. "We are most impressed," he concluded.

Zeno answered with a pleased smile and a humble nod.

"My Lord's pleasure is my delight," Cleopatra replied.

Her quick mind cast about for yet another way to forge the partnership between Egypt and Rome. She realized exactly what she must do to win over Caesar completely—mind, heart, and soul. Without so much as a blink of a royal eye, she offered him one of the precious manuscripts as a gift.

A shocked silence fell over the Great Hall. The courtiers ceased their chatter. The fluttering peacock feather fans suspended in mid-air. Torches sputtered in their braziers, now the only sound to be heard. The library staff was so stunned they could hardly breathe.

"Oh, my dear, I could not possibly..." Caesar demurred. Ever the gentleman, he was well aware of the impropriety of accepting such a gift when it was first offered. The library staff heaved a visible sigh of collective relief.

But Cleopatra persisted. "Nonsense, my Lord, the library is at your disposal. No one is more deserving than Caesar. You must take this volume with you, I insist—and others as well. The jewel of Alexandria must shine for Rome's glory."

"My dear, you are much too kind, but it is quite out of the question."

"Great Caesar, you cannot refuse me without breaking my heart. The books are yours, take what you will. Let them grace your home so that each time you read them, you will think of Egypt and remember your humble servant with favor. I beg of you, Caesar, accept these books as a token of our esteem and a symbol of everlasting friendship between your country and mine."

"Well, since you insist..." Caesar surveyed the masses of scrolls and manuscripts piled high upon the library table and pictured them arranged along the shelves of his villa in Rome. In his mind's eye, he saw himself welcoming senators and statesmen from all over the world and heard their admiring *ooohs* and *ahhhs* as they surveyed the incomparable literary spoils of his conquered territories.

"Very well," he proclaimed, "I accept!" After all, he had refused twice. To reject the queen's generosity further would constitute a serious diplomatic blunder, would it not? Besides, who deserved such a gift more than the great Caesar himself?

Thus satisfied that the proprieties had been duly observed, Caesar began his journey from one section of the library to the next, selecting from numerous shelves—including a number from the sections on magic and the occult—to be boxed up and sent without delay for loading onto cargo ships bound for Rome.

And, as bad luck would have it, he chose the ones Mindy and Zeno had been looking at and desperately needed to finish searching through—the ones she was certain contained the spell she had been traveling through time to retrieve.

Disbelief swept through the ranks. The library staff, along with Mindy and Zeno, watched in utter despair. But there was nothing to be done. To question a royal order was to invite death.

Cleopatra clapped her hands with delight as chests were brought, packed, and carted away to the docks. By the time the queen and her guest left for the royal banquet hall, a pall of gloom had descended over the library.

Never in his wildest imagination did the Master of the Keepers of the Books dream that his queen would give away Egypt's treasures to a Roman barbarian. Never did the library staff pray more fervently to Serapis, lord of all the gods, that such a royal visitor would never darken their doors again. They trailed out one by one, leaving Zeno and Mindy alone amidst the manuscripts and the sputtering torches.

Neither of them spoke. What was there to say? The

documents were gone, and with them her last hope of finding the magic spell she needed. Unless...

"Did you find it?" she whispered.

"I did not have a chance to read everything," he said, shaking his head. "I was not expecting them to come until after dinner. If we had had a little more time..." His voice then trailed off dejectedly.

She sank into the nearest chair and covered her face with her hands. This was the end of the road. She had failed her quest, made this whole journey, and worried her family out of their minds for nothing. The spell was lost because Cleopatra had chosen to impress Julius Caesar.

Zeno patted Mindy on the shoulder. "It is not your fault. Everyone knows the queen is unpredictable. There is not anything you could have done."

"Maybe not. But that's not going to be much comfort when Roxie gets her computer fixed. Do you have the slightest idea...?" But of course he didn't. How could he possibly understand the magnitude of what had just happened?

"No, I guess not. I was just thinking that if we could get to the docks, we might yet have time to go through the chests. Everybody will be at the banquet tonight. The books probably will not be loaded until tomorrow morning. It is a long shot, but it will not hurt to try."

"How long does it take to get to the docks from here?"

"To transport all the books, over an hour. But travelling on foot with nothing heavy to carry, we could get there in a fraction of the time. We could even take a chariot and be there in fifteen or twenty minutes."

She jumped up. "What are we waiting for? Let's go!"

But Zeno stopped. "Wait!"

A solitary figure had appeared at the other end of the room and began calmly re-shelving manuscripts. There was such pained resignation on his face as he lifted each one that Mindy wanted to cry.

But Zeno let out a joyous shout. "Eusebius!"

The man started. Then his smooth, ageless face broke into a radiant smile. He rushed to embrace Zeno as if they were long lost friends. He was obviously a man of considerable dignity and status, because Zeno sank to one knee and bowed his head.

"Eminence, I have no words to express my grief," he said. "What could we have done?"

"There was nothing, my son," the man replied wearily, bringing Zeno to his feet. "The blood of the gods flows in Cleopatra's veins. We cannot defy her wishes. But tell me, how came you to the library tonight? We were not expecting you until the morrow. By the gods, it is good to see you!"

"Thank you, Eminence, it is good to be home. The seas were clear and the winds behind us. We arrived in port a day early. Are you sure there is nothing we can do?"

"Quite sure. We can only pray that someday, somehow, the books will find their way back home here again. Meanwhile, the hour grows late, and I now have no stomach for a royal banquet. Tell me about your time in Greece. Is your family well?"

"They are well, Eminence. In fact," he said, motioning Mindy forward, "I have brought one of them back to Alexandria with me. This is my cousin, the Lady Mindora. Mindy, this is Eusebius of Tyre, Master of the Keepers of the Books. My mentor," he added proudly.

"And this is the young lady with whom Caesar spoke this afternoon. I am sorry, Lady Mindora, that your first visit to our beautiful city comes at such an unhappy time."

"I'm sorry too," she said. "It must be terrible for you."

"Indeed. But the sight of your bright, young faces cheers me immeasurably. We have missed you, Zeno. Your cousin," he explained to Mindy, "is a most capable and delightful young man. Somehow the library does not seem the same when he is gone. I have an idea. I want you both to join me for dinner in my chambers."

"That's very kind of you," Mindy began, "but we have to..."

Zeno interrupted. "We would be honored, Eminence. If you would allow us a few moments to refresh ourselves, we will join you directly."

"Excellent. I will tell my servants to set two more places. In a few moments, then." He bowed and disappeared silently into the shadows.

Mindy turned on poor Zeno like a raging banshee. "Why did you do that? We have to get to the docks right away!"

"I am truly sorry, but it would be unthinkable to refuse

Eusebius under the circumstances. His heart is broken, and he is like a father to me. Besides," he added, "I do not know about you, but I am very hungry."

"But..."

"Do not worry, the books will not get to the docks for at least an hour and will not be loaded on to the ship until morning. We have plenty of time."

CHAPTER SEVENTEEN

LAKE MAREOTIS

Mindy and Zeno didn't reach the docks until long after sundown. Across the harbor, even as the perpetual fire of the lighthouse threw its beacon out to sea, an ominous red glow hovered in the sky above the port.

The closer they came to the waterfront, the louder the sounds of shouting and the crackle and pop of burning wood became. People were fleeing in all directions, screaming and pushing each other out of the way. By the time they got there, the warehouse, depots, and granaries all along the length of the wharf were engulfed in flames.

Beyond the burning buildings, Ptolemy's war fleet, some sixty ships riding at anchor in the dark waters of the bay, were also ablaze. A gusty wind blowing inland from the sea had pushed some of the vessels closer to the shoreline and the sparks from their riggings had jumped quickly from the ships to the docks.

A human fire-brigade of hundreds of slaves was hastily passing buckets of water from hand-to-hand under the cracking whips of the harbor masters, but it was no use. Though the marble homes and public monuments of Alexandria were built over an elaborate network of underground cisterns that protected them from fire, the wooden docks were as dry as kindling.

Whipped by the wind, the flames spread like meteors along the rooftops, destroying everything in their path. Looting had broken out on the docks. Alexandria's citizens were making off with as much booty from the burning storehouses as their arms could carry—crates of squawking chickens and ducks, vats of wine and oil, tusks of ivory, and bolts of fine cloth. No one paid the slightest attention to the two young people who had just arrived at the terrifying scene.

"Zeno, look!" Mindy shouted as an old woman rushed by with her arms full of manuscripts.

He grabbed her by the sleeve. "What has befallen here, Ancient One?"

"Exactly what should happen, if you ask me. General Achillas has raised an army of twenty thousand against Cleopatra—former slaves, cut-throats, and Macedonians, to be sure, but an army nevertheless. His troops have taken over the palace, and now the mighty Caesar is a prisoner in his own love net, and his fancy Macedonian mistress with him. The general's troops sneaked right in during all the fancy goings on. Serves them right, trying to take the throne from young Ptolemy, flaunting their wealth in front of decent, hard-working folk, spending our taxes on all manner of foolish things."

"But the ships..."

"Never mind the ships, there are books on the docks—thousands of 'em. They will fetch good money in the marketplace. If you had the sense the gods gave a goose, you would grab as many as you can and stop bothering me. Now if you do not mind, I have better things to do than stand here jabbering with the likes of you." She squinted myopically at Zeno and snorted. "Humph. You look like one of them noblemen. If I were you, young man, I would look sharp. There is danger in the city for your kind tonight." She hitched up her books under her arm and disappeared into the crowd.

After questioning several more people, Mindy and Zeno were finally able to piece the story together. It seemed that Caesar had been in his seventh course at dinner—sweetmeats exquisitely seasoned with the finest spices from Asia—when a servant whispered news of a rebellion into his ear. He pushed his way past the dancing girls to the edge of the broad, flower-strewn terrace, where a sweeping view of the harbor confirmed the worst. His small navy was surrounded and completely outnumbered.

"Burn them!" he had shouted. "Burn every battleship in the Egyptian fleet!"

Chairs scraped back, banquet tables with their lavish

platters of exotic foods and pitchers of fine wines were overturned, and the lords and ladies of the court scrambled for safety.

Cleopatra had taken refuge in her chambers.

In the ensuing chaos, Caesar had escaped in a rowboat to Pharos Island where he set up headquarters in the lighthouse and waited for reinforcements.

Chaos reigned. The city was in revolt and its citizens were in an ugly mood. Anyone known to have come from the palace was suspect.

Zeno grabbed Mindy's hand. "We have to get out of here, fast!"

"Why? We haven't done anything!"

"It does not matter. No one will believe us. Let us go."

"Where?"

"North, through the Sun Gate. There is a ferry that will take us across Lake Mareotis. From the other side, we can escape into the northern desert. Come on!"

The smoke was so thick that Mindy could barely see, so she clung to Zeno's hand and followed, stumbling down the broad boulevard that led through the old Egyptian quarter. All around them were camels and carts filled with panic-stricken Alexandrians, jostling and pushing their way out of the city.

Zeno and Mindy passed over bridges and aqueducts, past the fabulous tombs of the Necropolis, and kept running until they arrived at last at the Temple of Serapis.

"The home of the smaller 'daughter' library," Zeno

explained to her.

"You mean there are more books in there? Let's go look!"

"There is not time. If the revolt succeeds, this place will be crawling with soldiers!"

As she watched the graceful porticoes of the temple disappear in the distance, she saw her hopes of finding the magic spell growing smaller and smaller.

They passed through the Sun Gate and emerged outside the walls of the ancient city where a path led to the marshy shores of Lake Mareotis. A man sat on the shore, his head down, asleep.

When Zeno tapped him on the shoulder, the grizzled old ferryman, with several teeth missing in front and a dirty turban wrapped around his head, stood up and motioned them aboard his raft. It was a small craft with low sides fashioned of reeds lashed haphazardly together.

Mindy looked from the raft to Zeno and back again, and shook her head. "It doesn't look very seaworthy."

"I know, but I have ridden this before and it is quite safe. Here," he said, dropping a few coins into the ferryman's upraised palm. "I will pay you the rest when we get to the other side."

The old man nodded, pocketed the money, and signaled for them to sit. As soon as he pushed off from the sandy bank, the current caught the raft and carried them quickly out into the dark waters of the lake.

On the far shore, barely visible under the pale light of

a round, low-hanging moon, Mindy could see the outlines of the dunes of the northern desert.

The same brisk wind that had blown the burning ships into the docks whipped the surface of the lake into frenzied peaks that pummeled the raft like a toy boat.

"I think I'm going to be seasick," Mindy groaned.

"Keep your eyes on the horizon and take long, deep breaths. We will reach the other side in a few minutes," Zeno reassured her.

Mindy liked the way he talked to her and seemed to genuinely care about her wellbeing. It made her feel special and important, as if she *mattered.*

Then a large wave hit the raft and tilted it heavily to one side. The boatman cried out. "Th...the...there!" he shouted, pointing a shaking finger. "Over there. I se...see...saw something in the water."

"I do not see anything," Zeno stated, narrowing his eyes and scanning the lake. "It was probably just a...gods help us!"

Mindy followed his gaze across the white-capped waters, and then she saw it too—a dark, rolling thing propelling swiftly through the water with the slithering motion of a snake. It was huge, at least ten times longer than the raft, and when its back broke the surface, the moonlight glanced off rows of reddish-black scales.

The creature raised its head above the water and surveyed the raft through a single, bulging copper eye, sizing the travelers up like a predator stalking its prey. Then it dove beneath the surface, leaving a phosphorescent glow in its wake.

"Where did it go?" Mindy asked frantically.

"I do not know. I cannot see anything," Zeno whispered back, fear creeping into his voice.

They waited. Behind her, Mindy could hear the old man's ragged, labored breathing.

"Look out!" cried Zeno.

Another wave hit the craft broadside. They clung to the sides as the raft almost upended and then miraculously righted itself again.

Then the beast re-emerged, even closer this time, a foul-smelling, sticky substance spraying from its nostrils.

The boatman sprang into action. He grabbed his pole from the bottom of the raft and lunged straight at the creature's eye. The pole hit its mark, and the beast writhed in pain as it slipped beneath the waves in agony. The old man breathed a sigh of relief and continued transporting his charges across the water to the opposite shore, hoping to reach land before anything else could go wrong.

The moon rose higher in the sky. Lake Mareotis basked silent and serene as the wind died down. Wavelets lapped softly against the sides of the raft, coaxing it toward the shore where the current pulled it into its welcoming arms.

Zeno gave the old man the balance of their fare, and then they stepped ashore on the golden beaches of the northern desert. They were shaking with cold and fear as they watched the old man and the raft pull away. Then they collapsed, exhausted, on the sand. The stars of the Milky Way sprinkled the shadowy dunes with a ghostlike, silvery light.

The night closed comfortably around Mindy and Zeno as the warm wind caressed their skin and dried their clothing. Neither of them said anything for a long time.

Finally Zeno sat up. "Are you all right?"

"Yeah, I think so. How about you?"

"I am fine. Look, Mindy, I am truly sorry we did not find your magic spell. I know how disappointed you are."

"It's all right," she said. "It wasn't your fault. I guess I should go home...only I wish I didn't have to go back empty-handed. Without the magic spell, I can't use the crystal ball, and there's nothing to stop Roxie."

"You did everything you possibly could."

There was a long silence.

"What are *you* going to do now?" Mindy ventured.

"I think I will follow the Nile upriver to Thebes and wait there until it is safe to go back to Alexandria. I have some relatives there I can stay with. I should probably leave now while it is still cool enough to travel. The sun will be coming up soon. What about you?"

"Well," she said slowly, "I suppose there isn't much point in hanging around here anymore."

Zeno stood up, clasped his hands behind his back, and looked down at his feet. "Mindy, I was thinking..."

"Hey, Zeno, I was wondering..." she said at the same time.

They both laughed.

Suddenly, a strange look came over Zeno's face. Slowly he pulled something out of his belt and held it up for Mindy to see. It was a scrappy piece of paper all wadded up.

"I nearly forgot all about this," he said, flopping back down on the sand and unfolding the paper across his knees. It was still wet around the edges, and some of the characters were smudged, but it was still readable.

"What is it?" Mindy asked half-heartedly.

"It is a page from a manuscript I found in the library. I did not have time to read it then, but it looked like it might be helpful, so I tore it out. Shall we read it now?"

"You took a page out of a manuscript?" Mindy asked incredulously.

"Well, yes, I..."

"You actually tore a page out of a book in the Library of Alexandria?"

"I did not know what else to do. You said there was someone coming, and...Do not be so shocked. I thought it might be important. I know how much finding the spell means to you, so I just..."

"Wow, you're the greatest!" Mindy threw her arms around Zeno's neck and tried to give him a big kiss on the cheek.

Zeno was so startled, he turned his head, and the kiss landed halfway down his neck, which startled Mindy in turn. They both blushed and started to laugh again.

When they finally stopped, Mindy leaned over Zeno's

shoulder while he read aloud. The letters jumped out at her from the page as if they were alive. Was it possible?

"Well? What do you think?" he asked.

"I can't believe it. Zeno, that's it! That's the exact spell I've been looking for all this time. Now all I have to do is take it back to India, read it aloud to Aggie, and we've won." Mindy looked at him in amazement. "And to think you had it in your pocket all this time!" She was so happy that she threw her arms in the air, tossed her head back, and shouted out, "Woooo-hoooo!"

Then the full magnitude of what had just happened hit her. Now there was no more reason to stay. In fact, the longer she delayed, the greater the danger. Mindy stopped in mid-shout and looked sadly down at Zeno.

"I have to go," she said softly.

He nodded. "I know."

He held out his hands and helped her to her feet, and they stood there staring at each other, not knowing what to say.

"So," Zeno said finally. "What is it like, travelling from one century to another?"

Is he stalling for time? "I don't really know. I mean, it's kind of hard to explain. First, I woke up under an olive tree in medieval Spain. The second time, when I escaped from the Cathedral of Toledo, everything started spinning, and the next thing I knew, I was sitting under an apple tree in Avalon. And the third time, when I shape-shifted into a seagull, I just started to fly, and by the time I landed in the rigging of your ship, it was over twelve hundred years earlier. It's always different. I don't have a clue what to expect this time."

Zeno whistled. "That is amazing. Nothing like that has ever happened to me. You know, I think you are the bravest person I have ever met," he said, taking both of her hands in his.

"I don't feel brave. It's more that I'm afraid of what will happen to my family and my friends—and the rest of the world—if I *don't* do something." She hadn't put it into words before.

"I know what you mean. But I still think you are incredibly brave."

"Would you consider coming with me?"

"No, I must stay here. The library is my destiny. I cannot leave it. I am really going to miss you, Mindy. I will never forget you."

"I'll miss you, too, Zeno."

Another silence.

"Right. Well, I guess we had better get started," he said abruptly. "Precisely how are you going to travel back to the twenty-first century?"

Mindy let go of his hands and looked up and down the beach. "I'm going to draw myself a magic circle, like Honi did, stand in the middle of it, and ask the Spirit of the Universe to take me home."

Zeno's eyes widened. "You know how to do that?"

"No, actually I've never done it before, and I'm not at

all sure I can do it now. But, you're not the only one who stole something from the library." She reached into her back pocket and pulled out the damp, bedraggled manuscript page. "I didn't have any way to copy it down, and I knew it might come in handy. See? All the symbols are right here. All I need is something to draw in the sand with."

Zeno ran to the water's edge and came back with two long, thin pieces of driftwood.

"Here," he said. "These are perfect. Where do you want the circle?"

"Far enough from the water so that the waves won't wash it away until we're done."

"All right, show me what to do."

Together Mindy and Zeno crafted a large, perfectly rounded circle and divided it into ten equal sections. With great care and precision, they filled in each section with the appropriate symbol according to the diagram, reciting the proper incantation as they completed each symbol. When everything was finished, they stepped back and surveyed their handiwork with mingled satisfaction and regret.

"It is beautiful, Mindy. Are you ready?"

"I...I think so. You'd better stand back, Zeno. I'm not sure what's going to happen next."

"Goodbye, Mindy. Good luck. Do not forget me."

"I won't forget you, Zeno—not ever. I promise."

Mindy looked around, taking it all in—the dunes, the moonlight, the wind-swept stars, her new friend. Then, she ran over and threw her arms around Zeno's neck. They hugged each other tightly. She kissed him gently on the cheek and whispered, "Thank you." Mindy then turned, walked over and stepped into the center of the circle, closed her eyes, and raised her arms, palms upward.

"Maker of the universe," she chanted. "You who hears all, sees all, and knows all, hear my plea. Take me home to India so that I may complete my mission and return to my family. And take good care of my friend, Zeno, wherever he goes. Maker of the universe, I will not move from this circle until you have answered me. Spirit of the earth, *hear my plea!* Spirit of the sky, *hear my plea!* Mighty ruler of the Middle Realm and all that dwells within and between— HEAR MY PLEA!"

Slowly, majestically, as if they had a life of their own, grains of sand began to rise, encircling Mindy like dancing spirits in a swirling golden curtain, until everything—Zeno, the moon, the beach—completely disappeared. The wind rose too, moaning and writhing. Softly flowing granules, sleek as silk, wrapped her in a gently rocking cradle. Beneath her closed eyelids, the light turned golden, then dark, then golden again. Strong arms scooped her up and held her safe, and without even opening her eyes, Mindy knew she was home.

PART FIVE:

PORTLAND, OREGON

AND

MUMBAI, INDIA

21ST CENTURY A.D.

CHAPTER EIGHTEEN

THE CRYSTAL TOWER

In the penthouse suite of the Crystal Tower, Roxie and Rasputin sat at her enchanted computer, ensconced once more in its place of honor on Roxie's desk, ready for the trial run of its newly installed, one-of-a-kind, state-of-the-art, magical software to begin.

"It's so good to have it back in working order. Now I feel like a real sorceress again," Roxie cooed.

"You always were a real sorceress, my Dark Angel," observed Rasputin. "I know how difficult these past few days have been for you, but now you can get back to being your adorable, malicious self."

"Thank you, darling, that's really very sweet. You know how much I appreciate your support. Wait until you see what this new software can do! I have the ability to destroy the entire Internet in a matter of minutes—which I have *no* intention of doing. Oh, no. I'm going to make the world *suffer* for the lost years these infernal machines have caused me, bit by agonizing bit. I'm going to rip the Internet apart piece by piece and watch it squirm. I'm going to invoke the most delicate tortures and confound every orderly system. Oh, it's going to be just delicious!"

Rasputin winced at her words but was able to convert his grimace into a smile just as she turned to look at him. "Well, what are we waiting for, darling? Let's get started."

"I thought you'd never ask. Watch this!" With a dramatic flip of her long curls, Roxie seated herself in the big, black leather chair facing her laptop and booted it up.

Then a message popped up on the screen:

Welcome, Roxie, to Chaos and Calamities, the newest, most powerful program in the realm of magic. All the forces of destruction are at your disposal as never before. You have only to command. To get started with your new program, please choose from the following menu:

> Internet
> Computer Viruses
> Court Systems
> Government Offices
> Banking
> Transportation
> Utilities

Wi-Fi

Stock Market

Communications

"This is going to be such fun," Roxie squealed. "Wherever shall we start? Let me see...they're all so perfectly potentially poisonous."

She moved the cursor over the list of categories with images depicting, in detail, a world dissolving into chaos.

"Computer Viruses," she read aloud. "Just the thing! I can start with one itty bitty little virus. Once I start spreading it to small businesses, I can move on to the big ones—corporations, manufacturers, even governments."

Her long, curved, fire-engine-red fingernail hovered over the mouse. Roxie paused, savoring the suspense, the drama of it all. She was in her element.

Besides doing evil deeds, there was nothing she loved more than being the center of attention. Finally, with great theatrical flair, Roxie brought her finger down.

Almost instantly—with a blinding flash and a thunderous BOOM that quaked the penthouse—the computer self-destructed, sending Roxie and Rasputin sprawling backward across the room.

The enchanted laptop shattered into a thousand pieces. Plastic, metal, and flames flew in all directions. The computer was nothing but a lopsided mass of molten parts, sitting forlorn and lifeless on the seared desk top.

On the other side of the room, Roxie sat in a stunned

heap, red hair singed and smoking, face blackened with soot.

Rasputin pulled her unsteadily to her feet. "My poor darling, are you all right?"

"Of course I'm all right," she snapped. "And for Heaven's sake, stop *fussing*. I'm perfectly capable of getting up by myself."

"Now *that's* the Roxie we all know and love," he exclaimed, infinitely relieved. "For a minute you really had me worried."

Roxie didn't answer. She wobbled over to the computer and stared down dejectedly at the shapeless gray mass.

"It's gone!" she wailed. "My one-of-a-kind, beautiful, fantastic, state-of-the-art, never-to-be-duplicated magic and sorcery software—gone, all gone. And, if I can't get my hands on that crystal ball, I'm through! Ruined. Defeated. Washed up. Forced into early retirement. Doomed to eke out the rest of my meager existence conjuring up petty spells and..." Her voice trailed off with a quiver of self-pity. A single tear squeezed out from under her long, black lashes, etching a sooty trail down her cheek.

"Come, come, my dear, that's positively ridiculous. Let's not grow melodramatic," said Rasputin briskly. "You're still a young woman, and a beautiful one at that, I might add. Your life is far from over. Chin up, darling, it's not the end of the world."

"But it *iiiiiiiiiis!*" Roxie sank limply into the only

remaining chair in the room. "Whatever shall I do now? I've been a sorceress for over a thousand years. I don't *want* any other profession. I can't go back to selling computers, I simply couldn't bear it. Sorcery is my LIFE!"

"Precisely the point, my dear, and a fascinating life it has been. That is why there is no better time than the present to retire and write your memoirs," he declared triumphantly. "I can see it now—the first sorceress ever to appear on the cover of *Cosmopolitan* and *Vogue*—the only sorceress in history to be interviewed on 'Ellen.' Why, you'll be so busy, you won't know what to *do* with yourself. Who wants to throw the world into chaos and bring back the 'glory days' from the past when there is so much fame and fortune to be had in the future?!"

"Do you really think I have a chance?" Roxie sniffled, brightening visibly. "I mean, do you honestly think my memoirs would sell?"

"My *dearest* Roxanne, of *course* they will sell! How many times must I tell you to have a little self-confidence...they will be an overnight sensation."

"I could call them, *A Day in the Life of Roxanne Evillovich.* It has a nice ring to it, don't you think? Very literary. Oh, Raspy, what a splendid idea! I'm simply astounded that I never thought of it before."

"*You* never thought of it? My dear Dark Angel, may I remind you..." Rasputin stopped himself in mid-sentence.

His plan to save Roxie from herself had worked, even though the computer had exploded instead of simply crashing—a bit *too* much emotion put into that spell, he supposed.

So, Rasputin wasn't going to complain if Roxie decided to take credit for it. The fact that she'd accepted his idea was good enough for him.

"What were you about to say?" Roxie asked, humming to herself as she rummaged for a pen and paper.

"Nothing, darling," sighed Rasputin, "nothing at all."

"Good, then it's settled. But, before I get started writing, there is one last item of business that I absolutely must take care of."

"And what is that, my Dark Angel?"

"That nasty little red-headed girl, Mindy what's-her-name. She's in India and Agamede is with her, and I want that crystal ball back! I shall have to go retrieve it. Be a dear and get this mess cleaned up while I'm gone, will you, darling? I'll be back in a jiffy."

"But darling, won't you be happy now without it? You led me to believe that you are moving on from the past and looking toward the future..."

Too late—Roxie was already gone.

CHAPTER NINETEEN

THE CONTEST

"Hurry up, Mindy!" Robert urged as he poked his head into her room. "I'm all done except for your part in my masterpiece. The judges are beginning their survey in one hour!"

Mindy was sitting on her bed. When she looked around, all the things in her room seemed to be right where she'd left them. "What judges?"

"What do you mean, what judges? For the Sandcastle Contest. Come on, Mins, we just talked about this last night. What's going on with you?"

The Sandcastle Contest. She'd forgotten all about it. "What day is it?" she asked.

"Sunday—all day."

"Very funny. It can't be Sunday, because..." *Wait a minute. Is it possible? Yes, it must be.* Robert hadn't asked any questions about where she'd been. So, if today was still Sunday, maybe time really had stood still while Mindy was gone, which meant that maybe it wasn't too late after all. But the clock was obviously ticking now.

Robert sighed. "What are you talking about?"

Mindy frowned, trying to collect her thoughts. Before she could reply, he rolled his eyes, grabbed her by the hand, and rushed her down toward the beach.

"But, Robert!" she protested.

He ignored her, and they hurried along until he sat her down on the sand chair he had already constructed. She barely had a chance to look at the sandcastle in all its glory.

"Don't move. In fact, can you just stay quiet while I work? I need to fix you up and do some finishing touches before the judges get here, and I really don't need any distractions."

Mindy obliged. She knew how important this was to her brother, and she didn't have the energy to fight with him.

After an hour of continual work, Robert deposited one last bucket of wet sand on Mindy's feet, tucked it neatly around her ankles, and fashioned a pair of dainty slippers with turned-up toes.

He pulled two ruby-red rhinestones out of his pocket and pressed one into the top of each slipper. Then he held his fingers in front of his face to form a square as if looking through the lens of a camera.

"Wow, this looks great! Stay still Mins, okay? The

judges will be here soon."

Robert brushed the sand from his hands and squinted at her. Mindy could tell he was having serious doubts about her mental health.

"Are you sure you're okay? You've had the strangest look on your face all morning," Robert queried.

"I'm fine. I just have a lot on my mind. I have a lot to tell you."

"Can you hold that thought? The judges are coming." He placed a bright turquoise turban on Mindy's head and stepped back to survey his handiwork. "Perfect!"

She looked down the beach. Sure enough, the judges were moving in their direction, stopping at each sculpture to jot down notes on their clipboards.

One of them, a young woman carrying the award ribbons in a basket, was extremely pretty, with alabaster skin and a tiny waist. She wore her hair pinned up against the heat, tucked beneath a wide-brimmed straw hat with black and purple ribbons around the brim.

What struck Mindy as rather strange was that she seemed more interested in looking up and down the beach than in inspecting the sandcastles. She wondered if the woman was searching for something, or someone. *What could it be?* Well, no matter. She had much more important things to think about right now.

"Robert."

"What?"

"I need to talk to you."

He sighed. "What is it now, Mins?"

"Uh, I don't quite know how to say this, but I have to go get Agamede right now."

"Agamede?"

"The crystal ball. That's her name, remember? I left her under the bed in my room."

"Look, Mindy Gayle," he said, using her full name the way their mom always did when she'd done something particularly bad. "I don't know what's gotten into you lately, but don't you think this crystal ball thing has gone a little too far? You've been acting really weird ever since it washed up on the beach. Maybe after the contest you should throw it back where it came from and forget about it."

"I can't. I'm sorry, there isn't time to explain it right now, but..." Gently as she could, she wriggled her toes just a little to see if she could pull herself out, but even the smallest movement sent thousands of tiny cracks scurrying in every direction.

"Don't you *dare* move! I worked really hard on this, and you're not going to mess things up for me."

"But, Robert!"

"No. This is so like you, Mindy. You start something, and then you just walk away and start something else—and you never think about what that does to other people."

"Like what?"

"Like Mom and Dad paying for all those swimming lessons, music lessons, dance lessons—and for what? For you to quit whenever you felt like it—whenever things started getting tough. You know what I think? I think you're afraid that if you ever learn to do something really well, you might not have any excuse *not* to do it anymore. Well, if you want to do that with your own life, that's fine, but I'm not going to let you ruin my chances of winning that mountain bike. The fishing float, or Agamede, or whatever you want to call it, is going to stay *right where it is* until the judging is over. And in the meantime, I don't want to hear another word about crystal balls or time travel or any of that crazy stuff, okay? Not one more word!"

Mindy blinked. She'd never thought of it that way before. But if she was completely honest with herself, she had to admit it was true, even if not in quite the way Robert thought.

It occurred to her, with one of those flashes of insight that was so embarrassing it made her cheeks turn red-hot even when nobody else was around—which was how Mindy knew she'd done something *really* stupid—that what she was afraid of was growing up. Maybe that was why she was so upset with Robert, because he was growing up, growing away from her, and she wanted *both* of them to stay kids forever.

That was when the truth hit her. There really wasn't anything Mindy could do to get her brother back, at least not the way she wanted. Whether he won or lost the Sandcastle Contest, he would still be more interested in girls and soccer than in hanging around with her.

But Mindy *could* find other things to do—like

completing her mission. Poor Robert! Instead of convincing her to see the Sandcastle Contest through to the end, he'd given her even more reason to finish what she'd started last Sunday in the bazaar with the cobra.

"Oh dear, what in the world do you suppose is going on over there?" asked Mrs. Fiddler, sipping lemonade under an umbrella with Ayah. She shaded her eyes with her hand. "Mindy and Robert seem to be having some sort of argument. That's odd, they almost never fight, or at least not until lately. Do you think it has something to do with the contest?"

"I'm sure I don't know, Missus." Ayah's eyes narrowed. "Perhaps I should go and see."

"Oh yes, please do," urged Mrs. Fiddler, setting down her lemonade. "No, wait, I'll come with you. I think it's almost time for the judging."

She started down the beach just as the judges were finishing their notes at the sculpture three entries away—a huge Bengal tiger with floral garlands around its neck.

Robert and Mindy glared at each other. Mrs. Fiddler looked at her children and sighed. She had grown up with six sisters. There hadn't been any boys in her family at all, not even cousins, until Robert was born. So when he'd turned into an almost completely different person seemingly overnight, she'd been utterly unprepared, even though her friends with teenage sons had warned her.

"I never thought it would happen with him," she'd told them. "He was such a sweet child, never any trouble, really. Now, all of a sudden, he's so moody, so *difficult*."

Her friends had nodded their sympathy.

"To make matters worse," she'd continued, "I haven't the *faintest* idea what to do with Mindy either. Sometimes I wonder if she'll ever apply herself to her studies and stop daydreaming. I suppose I should have another talk with her teachers. Thank goodness for Ayah! At least she gets them to listen, which is more than I can manage nowadays."

Looking around for the old woman, she saw with relief that Ayah had stationed herself solidly between Robert and Mindy. Mrs. Fiddler gave her a little wave, but the sun was in Ayah's eyes and she didn't wave back. Mindy's mother fanned herself with her hand. *If only the judges would get here!*

No one seemed to notice the cobra coiled in the sand at Ayah's feet, so perfectly camouflaged that it might have been a piece of driftwood left by the tide.

The fact that Ayah and her mother showed up at that particular moment was the last thing Mindy expected—or wanted. They would take Robert's side, of course, because they knew how badly he wanted to win and how hard he had worked to create the palace. If she so much as moved a muscle, there would be a huge scene.

Once she was confident that Mindy would stay put, Ayah rejoined Mrs. Fiddler on the sidelines to await the arrival of the judges. The "driftwood" remained.

Little droplets of sweat ran down Mindy's neck as the sun beat down on the heavy satin turban. Her head began to throb and she closed her eyes against the glare. When she opened them again, Robert was repairing the last little cracks in his masterpiece.

He gave her a thumbs-up. "Don't move!" he mouthed.

Mindy had to admit the palace was impressive—no, in all fairness to Robert, not impressive—spectacular. It was one of the biggest, most elaborate creations on the beach. It stretched out for ten feet in all directions, with guard stations at regular intervals along its crenulated walls, and a central courtyard with graceful arches around all four sides. He had decorated the courtyard with plants, and recreated the delicately carved screens where the purdah ladies used to sit, unseen, and watch the court comings and goings.

By this time, the judges had left the tiger and were only one entry away. They began to circle it and take down notes—all of them, that is, except the young woman carrying the ribbon basket, who was still anxiously scanning the beach.

She's even prettier up close, Mindy thought as the woman turned in her direction.

Then the woman froze. Slowly, ever so slowly, she

raised a small, white hand with perfectly manicured, fire-engine-red fingernails, and removed her sunglasses to stare unblinking as a cat. What was she looking at? Then the woman's gaze dropped and she saw Mindy.

A chill went down Mindy's spine, despite the glaring Indian sun. The woman's lovely, tip-tilted eyes took her in from toe to turban and changed slowly from russet-brown to a menacing amber. Suddenly Mindy knew, beyond the shadow of a doubt who she was. Neither of them moved.

"Psssst, Robert!"

"Get ready, Mins, they're coming!" He was so excited he was practically jumping out of his skin.

"I know. Just tell me one thing. The crystal ball—I mean the fishing float—where is it right now?"

"Behind you."

She looked around and caught the blinding flash of sunlight glancing off a glassy-smooth surface. Sure enough, perched like a shining jewel atop the highest domed tower of Robert's sandcastle, was the crystal ball, where he had placed it for all the world—or at the very least, the entire west coast of India—to see.

"Robert, why didn't you tell me?! How could you...?"

"Step back, please," interrupted a stentorian voice. "Ladies and gentlemen, please step back, so that the judges may get through."

A dignified, elderly gentleman with an enormous white handlebar moustache elbowed his way through the crowd and stopped directly in front of Mindy. He consulted his clipboard. "Now let me see," the gentleman began. "This entry is by Mr. Fiddler, is it? Yes, here it is, Robert Fiddler, number thirty-two. My, *my*, what have we here? Ah, the Purdah Palace at Jodhpur. An admirable effort, Mr. Fiddler, *very* nicely executed indeed! You must have gone to considerable trouble to build all this."

Robert beamed. "I did do a little research," he admitted modestly. "I wanted it to be as authentic as possible."

"And so it is," observed the judge, turning to the rest of the judges with an appreciative nod. "Most impressive."

All of the judges huddled together and whispered enthusiastically. After a few minutes, they broke apart, and the head judge drew a large, blue, first-place ribbon from the basket on Roxie's arm and handed it ceremoniously to Robert.

"I think we all agree that this is most definitely the best of show. Congratulations, my boy!"

The crowd burst into wild hoots, whistles, and applause. A dozen cameras clicked and whirred.

Mindy's mother looked as proud as one of the peacocks on their lawn. Even Ayah's usually expressionless face was wreathed in a smile.

They walked over to congratulate Robert, took some pictures, and then turned to head home and out of the heat of the day. Ayah paused and turned to look at Mindy with an enigmatic smile on her lips.

You know about Agamede, don't you? Mindy suddenly realized.

Of course, Ayah's eyes answered with a merry glint. *The magic of India helped you begin your quest, and it will help you to complete it. Have faith, Mindy, and believe in yourself.* And she quickly turned to follow after Mrs. Fiddler.

Mindy had heard Ayah's words in her mind, just as those with magical powers had heard her thoughts during her journey back through time, and they gave her strength.

Robert wanted to stay and admire his work of art for a while longer and forbade Mindy to move, despite her objections.

As the crowd began to disperse, the cobra stealthily moved through the sand toward Agamede. Soon, the only spectator left was Roxie, standing stiff as a statue, her eyes glued on the crystal ball.

What happened next would always be a blur in Mindy's mind. She heard Roxie's seething voice through clenched teeth mutter, "You stole my crystal ball, you wretched brats!"

"Agamede!" Roxie called, pointing her red-tipped finger straight at the crystal ball. "You will not escape me now! I call you to my service. Your will and your powers are mine to command. Come forth!"

"Mindy, no!" Robert shouted.

Too late. She had already shattered the throne to bits. Snatching the turban off her head, Mindy pushed through the wet sand, knocking over walls, screens, and plants, to reach Agamede perched atop the tower.

With a howl of rage, Robert lunged after her. At the

same time, Roxie flew through the breach. When they reached the tower, Mindy found herself trapped between Robert and Roxie as she stood her ground, blocking access to Agamede.

"You've nowhere left to go, my darling. Now, hand over the pretty little glass ball. It's an...uh...family heirloom. It's of no use to you—just of sentimental value. But it is *mine*, nonetheless, and I want it returned to me this instant!" Roxie snapped.

"Yeah, right," Mindy retorted. "Nice try. I know who you really are, and I know what you plan to do with Agamede. But I won't let you have her!"

"Don't test my patience, child. Hand over my crystal ball *immediately*."

When Mindy shook her head, Roxie clenched her fists and stormed toward her.

Fearing for his sister's safety, Robert stepped between them. "Wait..." he began in a calm voice." Mindy, maybe you should just give her the ball...I mean, she seems pretty serious."

"Yes, listen to your brother," Roxie cooed as she pushed Robert aside and stood face-to-face with Mindy.

Before Mindy could respond to either of them, without warning, the cobra Mindy had met at the bazaar, how long ago—it seemed like another lifetime—reared beside Roxie, its black and gold hood spreading wide.

Roxie froze in her tracks as the snake wrapped itself tightly around her leg. "Get off me, you wretched creature!"

she shouted.

"Move, and I shall bite," the cobra hissed at Roxie. Then he locked his eyes on Mindy's. "Namaste," the snake addressed her, bowing its head exactly as it had done that afternoon at the bazaar. "Greetings, Young Mistress."

"Namaste, Golden One. How did you know I was here?"

"Agamede summoned me—but it drains much of her power to do so. For that reason, I am only asked to come when I am truly needed. You have done well, Young Mistress."

"I...I hope so. Without your wisdom and faith in me, my quest would never have been possible. Your words gave me the courage I needed. How can I ever thank you?"

"If you believe in yourself and use your power wisely and only for good, then I shall be content. Namaste, my child."

"Namaste." Mindy brought her palms together and bowed once more.

Infuriated, Roxanne started to move, but the cobra hissed up at the sorceress, reminding her to stay in place.

Then, the crystal ball began twisting and stretching, stretching and twisting, like molten taffy. When she had completed her transformation, Agamede looked Roxie straight in the eye and calmly crossed her arms.

"So, Roxanne Evillovich," she began in her strange little voice, "we meet again. After being locked in a warehouse for centuries, I thought you had finished with me. What is it you want, Evil One?"

"Don't be insubordinate," snarled Roxie. "It was only a few centuries, more or less. And now, I have plans for you to help me put a little project into effect, which I expect you to do efficiently and cheerfully. And remember, were it not for the Evillovich clan, you would still be nothing but a few grains of sand in some desert. Now then," she said as she pointed at Mindy, "I want you to bundle up this arrogant child and her brat of a brother and cast them both into the sea. Preferably weighted down."

"These two?" Agamede's tinkling laugh sounded. "My dear Roxanne, you can't be serious. I couldn't possibly. Why don't you do it yourself? Better yet, why don't you have your fancy, high-tech enchanted computer do it? Much more efficient, I should think."

"Do you dare *defy* me, you insolent, traitorous little glass trinket? After everything I've done for you?!"

"Oh for Heaven's sake, Roxie. You seem to have forgotten to *formally* summon me while *holding* me as a crystal ball in your hands. Therefore, I do not have to obey a single command from you."

Roxie's mouth dropped open.

Before she could say another word, Agamede turned to Mindy. "Welcome home, my dear. I trust you had a pleasant journey. Did you find the spell, perchance?"

"Yes," Mindy replied. "You can't imagine what I saw and did to get it, but I have it right here in my pocket."

She glared at Roxie as she pulled the scrap of paper out and walked over to Agamede, who had morphed back into her cylindrical form. Mindy gently took the crystal ball in her hands, leaned into it, and whispered the magic spell.

"NOOOOO!" Roxie knew that without Agamede's power, she would never be able to execute her evil plan.

The cobra let loose its hold and moved away from Roxie—but it remained poised in case the sorceress attempted to attack Mindy.

Roxie wailed and fell to her knees.

Agamede stretched and twisted back into her humanoid form and smiled. "Well done, child. Your mission is complete. I am now in your service. What would you have me do?"

"Well," Mindy began, "let me think..."

BOOM! Mindy was interrupted by a loud, thundering rumble. A cloud of mist completely surrounded them.

When it cleared, a man stood in its place. He had curly black hair, a beard, and a moustache. His fingers were adorned with rings of onyx and moonstone, and he was wearing a purple cloak.

"R—Raspy?" blurted Roxanne as she scrambled to her feet.

"Hello, Roxie. I see things did not go as you planned?"

"No," she snapped. "How did you find me?"

"I used my supernatural item tracking system to locate the crystal ball. I figured I would find you near it. Oh, do forgive my terrible manners," he added, addressing Mindy and Robert. "I am Rasputin von Brunberg, sorcerer and computer expert, and longtime friend of Roxanne

Evillovich." He bowed at the waist, holding one arm across his stomach and extending the other out to the side, horizontal to the ground.

"N—nice to meet you," they stammered in unison.

"I was hoping to reach Roxanne in time," Rasputin explained, "before things got too terribly out of hand. I presume that Agamede is no longer in Roxie's power?"

"No, she is in my service now," Mindy answered proudly. "Mr. Brunberg, I don't mean to be rude, but why exactly are you here?"

He chuckled. "A very relevant question indeed. I had a sneaking suspicion that Roxie would be in need of some support if things didn't work out the way she desired."

"You decided to come to my aid NOW?!" Roxie screamed. "Well, you're too *late*, Rasputin. The little redhead got away with stealing my crystal ball—just like I feared. Whatever shall I do now?" she sobbed.

"My Dark Angel," he consoled her, "do not fret. Remember your plan to retire and write your memoirs? I would be most happy to assist you in your...career transition."

"Oh, Raspy," Roxanne said as her voice softened, "would you truly?"

Mindy frowned, perplexed. One minute, Roxie was ready to destroy the world—and the next, she was agreeing to retirement? *I must've missed the memo*, she joked to herself.

Mindy, Robert, Agamede, and the cobra watched as

Rasputin wrapped Roxie and himself in his large, purple cloak. Then, with a smile at Roxanne and a polite nod to the others, he pulled the cape tight, muttered an incantation, and the two of them vanished. In their place, a misty cloud shimmered in the Indian sun.

"Wow!" Robert exclaimed. "Didn't see that one coming."

"Me neither," Mindy agreed. "Thank you, again, Golden One," she uttered as she turned to the cobra. "You have perfect timing!"

"You are very welcome, Young Mistress. But, now my work here is done, and I must bid you goodbye. Namaste." Then he slithered off down the beach.

"Namaste!" Mindy cried and waved after him. Then it hit her. "We won!" she shouted in excitement.

"My most sincere congratulations," Agamede declared. "Now, you have a story to tell us, do you not?"

"Multiple stories, actually," she giggled. "You won't believe what happened! It all started when I woke up sitting next to an olive tree in medieval Spain…"

"Mindy, I'm so sorry," Robert said. "I should've been more supportive of you this whole time. If I had known what you were going to go through—wow, I'm a horrible brother! If I had believed you in the first place, then I could've gone with you and protected you! The angry mob, the fire, the sea monster...why did I let you go alone?"

"Robert," Agamede interjected, "you must remember that *I* sent Mindy on this journey. She had a valuable lesson to learn about the power of believing in herself. Do you truly think I would have sent her somewhere that her life would be endangered?"

"Aggie's right, Robert. If you had been there leading the way and protecting me the whole time, I never would have discovered things on my own. My adventure back in time helped me realize so much about myself—I really *do* have my own magic!"

"Speaking of magic, you still have not answered my question, Miss Mindy," Agamede's little voice chimed in. "Now that I am in your service, what would you have me do?"

A million things flashed through Mindy's mind at once. She thought of what it would be like to have her very own crystal ball, ready to help her any time she asked. She remembered what Don Lorenzo had said about how believing in one's self is the most powerful magic there is. She looked out across the water to where the seagulls were dipping and whirling, silhouetted against the bright blue sky. Everything was moving, yet at the same time, everything seemed to stand still.

"Nothing, Aggie," Mindy replied. "You have earned your freedom. I release you."

A single crystalline tear rolled down Agamede's cheek as she silently mouthed, "Thank you." Then she hurtled past

Mindy across the sand to the shoreline, dove headlong into the surf, and headed straight out to sea.

By the time Agamede finally bobbed up, having transformed into a crystal ball once more, all Mindy could see was the sun glittering off her crystal surface. Powerful currents enfolded her in their welcoming arms and carried her toward the far horizon.

CHAPTER TWENTY

ZACH

"Are you sure he's really that good?" Mindy asked for the hundredth time as she and Robert walked across the school lawn toward the computer lab. "I want this to be really special."

"Of course I'm sure. I keep telling you, this guy's a genius. He's been designing websites for a couple years now. He knows everything there is to know about them. I believe in him," Robert assured her.

As they walked in the lab door, Mindy was too busy pulling notes out of her backpack to notice the person, about Robert's age, who got up from one of the computers and walked over—until he was standing right in front of them.

"Hi, Zach, how's it goin'?" Robert greeted him. "Mindy, this is Zachary, the guy I was telling you about. Zach, meet my sister, Mindy."

He offered his hand. "Hello, it's really nice to meet you. Robert has told me a lot about you—all good stuff," he chuckled.

Mindy looked up. The way he carried himself, his eyes, his smile...*Impossible.* He looked *exactly* like Zeno. She tried hard not to stare. "Nice...nice to meet you," she stuttered, taking his outstretched hand.

A shock wave ran from the top of Mindy's head to the tips of her toes, and she turned a little pale. The grip was warm and familiar. Even the voice was the same!

"Hey, are you okay? Maybe you should sit down." Zach pulled out a chair, and Mindy sank into it as her knees turned to jelly.

Robert bent down and felt her forehead. "Hmmm. You're not running a temperature, but it is awfully hot today. Maybe you're not drinking enough water. Don't want to get dehydrated, you know. I'll go get you some."

"No, no, I'm fine, really. I just felt a little dizzy for a second," she called after him. But, he ignored her.

Robert came back from the cafeteria a minute later and handed Mindy a bottle of water. She gulped it down and set it back on the table so they wouldn't see that her hand was shaking.

"That's better. You had us a little worried there for a minute," her brother noted.

Zach smiled at her—that same sweet, familiar smile. Then he peered at her for a moment, and a strange expression came over his face. "You know," he said slowly, "somehow you look awfully familiar. Have we met somewhere before?"

"Sounds like a line from a corny old-time movie to me," teased Robert. "Uh, you guys seem to be getting along well, so if you don't mind, I gotta go check my locker and do some research in the library. I'll be back in an hour or so. Will that give you enough time to get this all figured out?"

Mindy and Zach exchanged looks.

"If it doesn't," Zach answered, "I'll walk Mindy home, if that's all right with her."

"Fine with me," she managed, trying to hide the shaking in her voice.

"Great. See you later." Robert shouldered his book bag and went out the door of the computer lab, whistling.

"So," Zach began, "let's get started. You know, I still can't figure it out, but somehow I'm just sure I've seen you before. In fact, I almost feel like I know you already. Weird, isn't it?"

"Very weird. Maybe if we don't think about it, it will come to us. Sometimes it happens that way," Mindy suggested.

"Yeah, you're right. Robert tells me you want to design a really fantastic website." He pulled up another chair. "What would you like to start with?"

"Camelot," Mindy replied.

THE REST OF THE STORY

Mindy Fiddler completed a Ph.D. in Computer Science. She now lives in England with her husband, **Zachary Zimmerman**, their two children, three dogs, two cats, and pet snake.

Zenodotus of Phaleron (Zeno) resided for fifty years as Master of the Keepers of the Books for the Library of Alexandria before retiring to an island off the coast of Greece. He was reincarnated in the twenty-first century as **Zachary Zimmerman** and created the world's largest online bookstore.

Robert Fiddler completed a Ph.D. in Electrical Engineering in the United States and returned to India to carry on his father's work.

Ayah returned to her village after the Fiddlers left India and married the snake charmer from the bazaar.

According to legend, **Honi the Circlemaker** fell asleep in the first century B.C. and woke up seventy years later. Of course, no one believed his story. On his 120th birthday, he drew himself a circle, stood inside, and disappeared into mythology.

Don Lorenzo Alejandro de Carpio retired to his country estate after the Department of Magic and the Occult was abolished. He was reincarnated in the sixteenth century as Domenikos Theotokopulos, the renowned painter, better known as El Greco. During the Renaissance, he enjoyed the fame denied him as a medieval scholar.

Roxanne Evillovich retired from practicing sorcery and wrote her memoirs. After a very successful tour of the lecture and television circuit, she returned to the West Coast to host her own talk show.

Rasputin von Brunberg was exceedingly impressed with Roxie's writing, as well as her willingness to finally adjust to the modern world. After centuries of uncertainty about her feelings for him, she said yes when Rasputin worked up the nerve to propose to her on live television.

Agamede resurfaced in China in the eighteenth century. Her sudden appearance so unnerved the wife of the Emperor of the Sun, that the Divine Empress...well, that is a story for another time.

ABOUT THE AUTHOR

 Gail B. Schwartz was born and raised in Portland, Oregon. She attended the University of Oregon, majoring in music, and spent a year in their music program in Oldenburg, Germany. During that time, she traveled widely in Europe. Her wonderful writing talent began showing up in the many beautiful letters she sent home. Gail earned a bachelor's degree in General Studies from Portland State University. She later spent a year in the music school at Hebrew University in Jerusalem, and during this time, she traveled around the Middle East. She received her master's degree from U.C.L.A. in Ethnomusicology with a specialty in Middle Eastern music and a minor in Arts Management. She worked as a grant writer and also taught grant writing at Portland State University. Gail moved to Los Angeles, where in addition to her business as a grant writer, she sang with a large women's choir. After twenty-two years in L.A., Gail returned to her native Portland. She lived there until she died from cancer in 2009.

Agamede, A Tale of Magic, was her first novel. The sandcastle contest in the story was based on her many visits to Cannon Beach, Oregon, and its annual sandcastle building contest. The book has been published in Gail's memory with permission from her sister, Linda Schwartz.